The Gold Smugglers

(original title: Patriots' Gold)

by VIRGINIA FRANCES VOIGHT

Cover by Ethel Gold

SCHOLASTIC BOOK SERVICES

NEW YORK • TORONTO • LONDON • AUCKLAND • SYDNEY • TOKYO

12 11 10 9 8 7 6 5 4 3 2 1   1   8 9/7 0 1 2 3/8

To My Sister Elizabeth

Contents

July 4, 1776

DAWN was painting the sky above Philadelphia with watermelon pink, when Sam Woodbury rolled out of his bed in the loft room above Leeds' Printshop. Mr. Leeds, the master printer to whom Sam was apprenticed, expected him to have the shop open and ready for business early in the morning.

The printer had been very busy with work during this summer of 1776. In addition to the regular book and job printing, there was work to be done for the Continental Congress, and in a day or so Mr. Leeds and the other printers of Philadelphia expected to receive the most important job of all.

Sam smoothed his sandy hair with a wooden comb and tied it at the back of his neck with a black cord. He pulled on his ink-stained breeches, picked up his shabby calico shirt, and ran down through the shuttered printshop to the garden that stretched between the shop and the Leeds' house.

A redbird was whistling clear and high from the top of the pear tree. Sam joined in with a cheery whistle of his own, as he drew a bucket of water from the well and filled the small wooden tub on the bench by the shop door. He splashed vigorously, a lean boy, rather short for his fourteen years, with a clean-cut good-looking face and intelligent gray eyes. He rubbed himself dry with his shirt and then rinsed the shirt in the tub and spread it on the wellcurb to dry. Quietly he let himself into the Leeds' kitchen.

Mr. and Mrs. Leeds were still abed, but Sam was accustomed to getting his own breakfast. In the foodsafe, he found a bowl of cold scrapple left over from supper. Taking this, a horn spoon, an earthenware mug, and a saucer, he went back to the garden. George, the big yellow tabby cat, who was all the family that Sam had in the world, was waiting expectantly. He greeted Sam with an eager *Meow*.

George had been with Sam for two years now, ever since Sam had found the scrawny lost kitten floundering in a snowdrift. They shared the loft room in winter, but in warm weather George preferred to spend his nights roaming the gardens and alleys of the neighborhood. Mrs. Leeds hadn't been enthusiastic about having a kitten added to the household, but in time she was forced to admit that George was a valuable mouser. She refused, however, to pay him in food for policing the premises, so Sam shared his own meals with his friend, and in return the cat brought him presents of dead mice, rats, and grasshoppers.

At first the kitten had been known only as Mouser, but he had grown up to be a notable warrior, able to lick the ears off any other cat who ventured into his territory. Last year Sam had named him George after the great soldier from Virginia who had been made Commander in Chief of the Army of the Thirteen United Colonies of America.

Sam filled the cat's saucer with scrapple. Then he poured milk into his mug from the jug set on a shelf inside the well, and ate his own scrapple.

By the time Sam had washed their dishes and opened the wooden shutters on the print-shop windows, the hot July sun had dried his shirt. As he buttoned it on, he noted that the bookshop at the Sign of the Red Goose Quill, just across Sassafras Lane, was open also. Sam gathered up an armful of pamphlets that Mr. Leeds had printed the day before and walked across the lane, with George padding along behind him. Inside the bookshop, George jumped up into the deep show window and stretched out between some music books and a copy of *Peregrine Pickle*.

Ellen Clay, who lived with her mother and her uncle in the little red-brick house attached to the bookshop, stopped dusting books to smile at the cat.

"Uncle Seth is always saying what a wonderful attraction George is for the shop," she told Sam.

She was a year younger than he, a cheerful girl with violet eyes and a gently curved mouth. She wore a pink cotton-print gown with a crisp white apron, and the mobcap that topped her lustrous black curls had a dainty ruffle of handmade lace.

"People stop to look at George," she continued. "And then they notice the books and come in to buy. He keeps the mice away too. Mice can do a lot of damage to book bindings. We ought to pay him wages." She chuckled softly.

"What about all the meals you hand out to him, and to me as well?" Sam replied. "I feel as if I ought to catch a few mice for you myself."

The Clays treated Sam as one of the family, and his lonely heart was grateful.

Two years ago Mr. Leeds had taken Sam out of an orphans' home, and the law had bound Sam firmly to the master printer for six years of apprenticeship. Mr. Leeds was a skilled craftsman but a hard master. Sam frequently put in fourteen hours a day at the shop, besides doing chores around the house. He was struck with a switch whenever Mr. Leeds felt that he was lacking in diligence, and he was given only the plainest food and little enough of that.

On the bright side, though, Sam was receiving a thorough training in a good trade, and Mr. Leeds, who was fair as well as stern, saw to it that he had time off in winter to go to school. At his eighteenth birthday, Sam would be free and have the right to call himself a full-fledged printer. He made many hopeful plans for that day.

While Ellen stacked the pamphlets on the counter, Sam lingered to stare hungrily at a table of books. "Will I ever have enough money to buy books?" he sighed.

"Wait until you're a rich master printer like Dr. Franklin," Ellen said. "He was in here yesterday. He told Uncle Seth that the Congress will probably pass the Declaration of Independence today."

Sam's eyes shone. "It's about time!" he exclaimed. Like Mr. Leeds and the Clay family, Sam was a staunch Patriot.

The war with England had been going on for over a year now. This summer, the question of whether the Thirteen Colonies should declare their independence was being hotly debated in the Continental Congress. And Sam had a special source of information on what was happening behind the closed doors of the State House; his best friend, Tim Monroe, was a government dispatch rider. So Sam knew that General Washington and a majority of the Congress had agreed finally on complete independence from England. It was, they felt, what the people of the Thirteen Colonies wanted and needed. Delegate Thomas Jefferson of Virginia had written a Declaration of Independence. Most members of the Congress were well pleased with it, but others were finding fault with the way it was written. The debates were continuing, while the Patriots of Philadelphia waited anxiously to hear that they had become citizens of a brand-new country.

Ellen walked with Sam to the bookshop door. "Here's Tim," she said. "Perhaps he has some news for us."

A tall jaunty youth was riding along on a fine black horse. He pulled up under the tree that shaded the bookshop and doffed his hat to

Ellen. Tim Monroe was two years older than Sam and liked to think he was a man of the world. His riding boots were rubbed to a high polish, and so was the leather dispatch case slung over his shoulder. The butts of two pistols protruded from the holsters on his saddle.

Sam walked over to the horse and stroked his nose. "Any news, Tim?" he asked.

His friend nodded. "Something's going to happen today for sure. All of us had orders to be at the State House early. When they pass the Declaration, express riders will carry printed copies of it to people all over the country. Dr. Franklin told me to stand ready to rush a written copy to Mr. Leeds. He is to print broadsides for me to carry to the towns north and west of Philadelphia. I wish I were going to New York with General Washington's copy," Tim added wistfully.

"I'd be glad to have your job no matter where I was going," Sam said enviously. "Even riding to the farms up the Schuylkill would be more exciting than running our creaky old press."

Tim flicked the reins. "Giddap, Chief! If they do pass the Declaration today, you'll be seeing me, Sam."

"Sam!" thundered a voice from across the lane.

"Coming!" Sam shouted back. With a hasty

7

wave of his hand to Ellen, he sprinted back to the printshop.

Mr. Leeds, a thin hawk-nosed man with stooped shoulders, stood in the doorway of the printshop, tying on his leather apron.

"Wasting your time talking to that girl!" he grumbled. "Have you cut the paper for those handbills?"

"Yes, sir," Sam replied. He took down his own worn and ink-stained apron and tied it on.

The printshop was a cluttered, untidy place smelling strongly of ink, paper, and leather. Piles of fresh paper and printed material were stacked on the shelves that lined the walls. Mr. Leeds' desk was littered with manuscripts waiting to be set in print. The cupboards overflowed with a jumble of supplies.

The most important pieces of furniture were the tall, wooden printing press and the type cases in which the lead numerals, letters, and points were kept. These cases were in perfect order. It was one of Sam's duties to put the types back after each printing job was finished, and to keep them clean and carefully sorted, each in its own compartment so that no time would be lost hunting for letters and numerals when a manuscript was being set in print.

"We'll set up the handbills that were ordered for tomorrow's auction," Mr. Leeds decided, after looking over the work on his desk.

There was a businesslike clink and rattle of type as he picked the letters and numerals he needed from the cases and arranged them upside down in his composing stick. When the stick was filled, he emptied it carefully onto the galley, a flat brass sheet with raised sides. A proof was taken from this with the proof press. Then the proof was checked carefully with the written copy of the auction bill. The master printer quickly corrected the few errors in the proof and then commenced the final printing of the handbills.

Sam had soaked two balls of wool and leather with ink. He used the balls to spread ink evenly on the type that Mr. Leeds had set up on the press. Then he took turns with his master swinging the heavy wooden handle that worked the press.

While they worked, the sun climbed high into the hot July sky and the air grew heavy and humid. Mr. Leeds' face was flushed and he was breathing heavily, but he kept on working until the last handbill was off the press. Then he fell into a chair and pulled out his handkerchief to wipe his damp face. "This heat is making me ill," he rasped.

Sam hastened to fetch a dipper of water

from the well. Mr. Leeds drank it slowly and then got unsteadily to his feet. "I'm going to lie down for awhile. Sam, take the wheelbarrow and deliver this work. Bring back five pounds of lampblack. We'll mix ink this afternoon."

Sam removed his apron and scrubbed his hands at the washbench with soft soap. He piled the still-damp handbills in the wheelbarrow and trundled them to the shop of the merchant who had ordered them. When he returned to the shop with the pot of lampblack in the wheelbarrow, he saw Ellen waving to him.

"Oh, Sam!" she cried, running across the lane to meet him. "Have you heard the news? Congress has passed the Declaration of Independence! A friend, who was at the State House when the vote was taken, came to tell Uncle Seth about it just a few moments ago."

"Hurrah!" Sam shouted. He dropped the handles of the wheelbarrow and took Ellen's hands in his. "Hurrah for the United States of America!" He danced her around in the street until her violet-sprigged petticoat flared out like a bell.

"I wonder if Mr. Leeds has heard the news?" Sam gasped.

"I don't know." Ellen was laughing and trying to catch her breath all at once.

"This will mean work for us tonight. Tim should be here any moment now with a copy of the Declaration. I'll see you, Ellen." Sam pushed the wheelbarrow hastily through the Leeds' gate.

It was strangely quiet at the printshop. And when Sam carried in the lampblack, he found the place deserted. He hung around uncertainly for a few minutes and then walked through the garden to the house. Mrs. Leeds met him in the kitchen with her fingers on her lips. "Don't make any noise! Your master is very ill. The doctor has bled him and now he must stay in bed and rest for several days."

"I'm sorry, ma'am," Sam said. "Can I do something to help?"

"Just stay out from underfoot."

Suddenly Sam remembered about the Declaration; he gave Mrs. Leeds a stricken look. "But Mr. Leeds just can't stay in bed!" he burst out. "The Congress voted for the Declaration today and Dr. Franklin expects Mr. Leeds to print — "

"Ben Franklin indeed!" Mrs. Leeds said crossly. "If he comes here, just tell him that Mr. Leeds is going to stay in bed until the doctor says that he can get up. Now go and tend the shop, and don't promise any work to *anyone!*"

She shooed Sam out of the house as if he had

11

been a stray cat. She had completely forgotten that he had not had any dinner, and Sam did not dare to remind her. He picked a handful of ripe strawberries from the garden and washed them down with a drink of milk from the jug in the well. George was nowhere about, so Sam guessed that Ellen had fed him.

In the shop, Sam mixed some ink. At least he could get things ready, in case Mr. Leeds should recover in time to print the Declaration.

Before the war, English law had required that the Colonists import all their ink from England, but now that they were cut off from this supply, Americans had learned to make ink for themselves. Sam mixed a varnish of linseed oil and rosin in a large stoneware crock and stirred in the lampblack. It was twilight before he finished the job, and he had just finished cleaning up when he heard a horse trotting along the lane. A moment later, Tim Monroe rushed into the printshop, waving a paper.

Sam Does His Part

"HERE you are, Sam!" Tim shouted. "The Congressional clerks have been wearing out their goose quills writing copies of the Declaration for the printers. But Dr. Franklin has seen to it that I have an early one for Mr. Leeds. Where *is* Mr. Leeds?" he demanded, glancing around the dusky shop.

"He's sick," Sam answered glumly. "He can't get out of bed."

"What?" Tim yelped. "But this work must be done tonight."

Sam took the closely written paper over to the door and commenced reading.

"In Congress, July 4, 1776.

The Unanimous Declaration of the Thirteen United States of America — "

Little chills chased one another up Sam's spine as he read on. When Tim twitched his sleeve, he looked up impatiently.

"You can read that later," Tim said. "Right now you've got to rouse out old Leeds! Dr. Franklin is depending on him to print hundreds of broadsides tonight."

Sam's grip tightened on the wonderful document that had made him the free citizen of a free country. It had taken a lot of courage for the men in Congress to vote for the Declaration of Independence, pledging their lives, fortunes, and sacred honor in the fight for liberty. They knew that if England won the war, every one of them would be hanged by the angry King. Now it was *his* turn.

Sam's jaw set in a firm line. "Don't worry, Tim," he told his anxious friend. "The broadsides will be ready when you come for them. I promise."

"I'll be here at dawn. I want to be the first express rider out of Philadelphia tomorrow. Don't fail me, Sam!"

"I'll be working this old press while you're snoring tonight."

Sam watched Tim swing up on Chief and ride away until the dusk swallowed the black horse and the jaunty rider. The printshop was dark and still and so was the bookshop across the lane. But there was a glow of light in the Clay house, where Ellen was lighting the candles in the hall and parlor.

14

A gentle breeze stirred the leaves on the trees that arched the lane. Here and there a star twinkled down. Suddenly Sam felt frightened and alone. What had he done? He had rashly promised to print hundreds of copies of the Declaration of Independence when he knew that Mr. Leeds was too ill to come to the shop and he must do the work alone — he who had never printed even a visiting card by himself!

Panic mounted inside him. He must have been crazy when he promised to do such a tremendous piece of work! Now he'd just have to walk over to the Monroe house and tell Tim he'd have to find himself another printer.

The quiet evening was suddenly split by a crescendo of yowls and caterwauling. There was a wild scurrying among the bushes in the Leeds' yard and more ear-tingling howls, then George's triumphant battle cry shivered to the stars. The big stranger tom cat, who had dared to invade George's domain, streaked past the printshop. A moment later, George came soft-footed out of the shadows to rub against Sam's legs and purr. Except for his swollen tail, he looked like a gentle fireside tabby.

"At it again!" Sam chided. "You never dodge a fight, do you, boy?"

Sam's shoulders straightened out of their

discouraged slump. Neither had Congress dodged the fight to declare independence. Nor was General Washington dodging the bitter, unequal struggle to make independence a living fact.

"And I'm not about to dodge my part in the fight," Sam muttered, clenching his fists. "I'll print the Declaration or die trying."

The voice of the Town Watch rang out, calling the hour as he lighted the lamp at the corner of the lane. Sam drew a deep breath. There was a long night ahead for Sam Woodbury!

He stepped into the dark printshop, felt for the tinderbox on the mantel over the fireplace and lighted a twist of paper. After he had lighted every candle in the shop, as well as two lanterns, he hesitated. Should he try to persuade Mrs. Leeds to let him see her husband? He knew the master printer had been waiting all summer for this important job, and would do it if he were able. At least he could tell Sam where to find someone to help. Then Sam let out a deep sigh. Instinct warned him that Mrs. Leeds would command him to let the work go. He had better go ahead by himself.

Fortunately there was plenty of paper on hand. He fetched sheets from the cupboard and cut them into the size he would need for the broadsides. He had just finished when Ellen came into the shop with a basket on her arm.

"Mama thought that Mrs. Leeds might not have time to give you supper tonight."

She cleared a space on the desk and spread a napkin for a tablecloth. From her basket she took a flaky little meat pasty, a jug of milk, and a generous wedge of cherry pie. She set down a saucer of milk and one of meat for George, who had followed her into the shop.

Ellen perched on a stool while Sam and George ate hungrily. Between bites Sam told her of his promise to print the Declaration of Independence. Her eyes shone.

"What a wonderful thing for you to do, Sam. But won't you need some help?"

He shrugged. "I can set the type alone. It's the handling of the press that worries me. It's heavy work. I hope my arms hold out."

Ellen jumped down from the stool. "Sam, you're going to have *two* helpers. Uncle Seth can spell you at the press and I'll do odd jobs. I'll tell Uncle that you need our help."

She ran out of the shop and across the lane to the Clay house. A smile brightened Sam's face as he looked after her. It was good to have friends!

He cleared away his supper dishes and pegged out Tim's copy of the Declaration on the desk. Moving a candle closer, he read the paper through carefully. Finally he took up Mr. Leeds composing stick and, with a hand that trembled a little, selected an *I* from the upper case of type.

"In Congress, July 4, 1776."

As he proceeded, Sam's nervousness vanished and he worked with confidence. This was going to be Sam Woodbury's contribution to the great day of independence, and it wasn't going to be any coarse blundering job, he told himself. He ran off the proof and was correcting it when Ellen returned with her uncle.

"What can we do to help?" the bookseller asked briskly, rolling up his sleeves.

Sam pointed to a tub of water. "The paper must be dampened."

He inked the type with swift, sure hands, then laid on the damp paper that Ellen handed him and ran the carriage under the screw. The power for making the impression was supplied by the screw. Sam swung the wooden handle with all his strength, determined that the printing should be sharp and clear. When he took the first broadside from the press he glowed with pride. Ellen looked over his shoulder. "Oh, Sam, that looks splendid!"

"Very nice work indeed," Mr. Clay agreed.

Sam returned to his work with a light heart. As the summer night wore on, the air in the printshop became heavy with the smell of ink, damp paper, and burning wax. Sam's wet face glistened in the candlelight as he pulled on the screw handle. Mr. Leeds had always declared that working a printing press took as much muscle as plowing a field, and Sam agreed with this heartily. After several hours he wondered why his weary arms didn't drop off. Mr. Clay took over every little while, but Sam did most of the work. He wanted it that way. He wanted this job to be as much his own as possible.

Ellen and her uncle helped with the inking, supplied damp sheets of paper as they were needed, hung up the printed sheets to dry as they came from the press, stacked the dry sheets in neat piles, and renewed the candles as they burned down in their holders.

Hours ago the candles in the houses along Sassafras Lane had been snuffed out, but in the printshop the press continued to creak and rattle as the screw came down and the carriage ran back and forth. The piles of printed broadsides mounted higher and higher.

The Watch, making his rounds, had just called out the hour before dawn when Sam took the last sheet from the press. Mr. Clay had fallen asleep in the chair by the desk, his powdered wig askew and his spectacles slipping down his nose. Ellen was heavy-eyed from weariness as she took the last sheet from Sam and pegged it on the line. Almost as if she were moving in her sleep, she reached out for another sheet. Sam's yell of triumph startled her wide awake.

"We're through, Ellen! We're through!"

He threw his arm around her shoulder and gave her a hearty hug.

"What's this?" Mr. Clay sat up and settled his wig. "Have you finished, Sam?" He took a sheet off the nearest pile of broadsides and peered at it closely. "No master printer could have done a better job," he praised.

Sam flushed with pleasure. "I couldn't have done it if you and Ellen hadn't helped me." Then he added thoughtfully, "After tonight, the Declaration of Independence will always seem to be truly mine."

Ellen gave him a warm glance. "Now you won't feel so much left out of things when Tim rides away on one of his trips."

Sam nodded, pleased that she understood how he felt.

"Well, Ellen, come along," said Mr. Clay. "Master Printer Woodbury has no further use for his helpers."

Sam followed his friends to the door and watched them cross the street in the dim morning light, Ellen smothering a yawn with a smudged hand. Birds were chirping drowsily in the branches overhead. Sam breathed deeply of the cool, fresh air of dawn. In spite of his tiredness, he had never felt so good in his life.

A clatter of hooves sounded on the cobblestones, then Chief came down the lane with Tim in the saddle. Tim pulled up the horse at the Leeds' gate and leaped to the ground. "Are you ready for me?" he asked eagerly.

Sam put on a doleful expression. "Mr. Leeds was too sick to work the press."

Tim stared at him. "You — you didn't print the broadsides?" he demanded hoarsely.

"Come and see!" Sam led his friend into the printshop and waved a hand toward the piled sheets. "Ellen and her uncle helped me print them."

Tim snatched up one of the sheets for a closer look. "Zounds! Old Man Leeds couldn't have done any better!" There was a new note of respect in his voice.

Sam grabbed one of the saddlebags that Tim had brought with him. "I'll help you pack them."

As he thrust a sheaf of broadsides into the bag, he thought with pride that soon hundreds of people would be reading copies of the Declaration of Independence that had been printed by Sam Woodbury.

They crammed the bags full, and Tim tied a sack of broadsides at the back of Chief's saddle. Then he swung astride the horse and gathered up the reins. "I'll be seeing you in a few days."

"Good luck!" Sam replied. "Don't run into any British or Hessians."

"If I do, I'll give 'em copies of the Declaration."

As Sam watched his friend ride away, weariness settled over him like a fog. He had just energy enough to blow out the sputtering candles and bar up the printshop door before stumbling up the ladderlike steps to his room. Kicking off his shoes and tossing aside his dirty apron, he threw himself down on the quilt that covered his bed. In a moment he was fast asleep.

Sam was in high favor in the days following his printing of the Declaration. Mr. Clay made sure Dr. Franklin knew that the boy had shouldered a man's responsibility. One day the Doctor, accompanied by Mr. Milton, another Philadelphia delegate to the Continental Congress, called at the printshop to congratulate Mr. Leeds on the ability of his young apprentice. Mr. Leeds could not but feel that all these praises reflected his own glory as a printer. He was so pleased with Sam that he gave him a new shirt and breeches, so that he would not look quite such a ragamuffin the next time he met Dr. Franklin.

Mr. Milton slipped Sam a gold dollar as a token of his approval. It was the first money of his own that Sam had ever had. He promptly spent some of it to buy a copy of Pope's translation of Homer's *Iliad*, which he had long been eyeing as it stood on a shelf in the bookshop.

The book remained a treasure to enjoy, but otherwise Sam's brief time of excitement soon passed and the old routine of hard, exacting work returned. Once more he sighed with envy for Tim's job of high adventure, and wondered if anything exciting would ever happen to him.

Sam Rides Into Adventure

WITH the coming of autumn the war moved closer to Philadelphia.

New York had been lost to the enemy and General Washington just managed to save his army by a masterly retreat across New Jersey into Pennsylvania. The Continentals crossed the Delaware River and left the British stranded on the New Jersey shore by gathering in all the boats for miles up and down the river and securing them on the Pennsylvania side.

With Washington's retreat into Pennsylvania, the American cause reached its lowest ebb since the beginning of the war. Congress had no money with which to pay and supply the troops, and so the army melted away until Washington was left with less than three thousand ragged, hungry men. Alarmed by the near approach of the enemy to Philadelphia, the Congress fled to Baltimore. The Tories of

Philadelphia began to say openly that it was all over for the Patriots.

Mr. Stone, an elderly Tory who lived next door to the Clay family, took great pleasure in dropping in at the printshop to predict that soon Mr. Leeds would be marched off to prison for his part in printing the Declaration of Independence. Once, the two neighbors had been friends, although they had always argued about politics. Now each considered the other to be a traitor.

One day when Mr. Stone was advising Mr. Leeds to leave town before Sir William Howe arrived to clap him into jail, Sam looked up with a frown from the bucket of type that he was washing.

"Twas I, not Mr. Leeds, who printed the Declaration," he reminded their Tory visitor.

"Tush!" rasped Mr. Stone. "You're but a boy. 'Tis your master who'll be held responsible, and rightly so. Not only because he himself is a traitor, but because he has influenced you to rebellion against your king."

"Take your sour face out of this shop, Thomas Stone!" Mr. Leeds roared. He brandished his composing stick. "If I have taught young Sam to cherish liberty, I'm proud to own it. 'Tis you who are the traitor to your country. But don't crow too soon! The Redcoats aren't in Philadelphia yet."

Mr. Stone backed toward the door. "They will be soon."

"Much good it will do for them to take the city if General Washington holds the country around it. And let me tell you, our Cause will never be lost while General Washington has a single American soldier to stand between his country and the rule of tyranny! Now get out of my shop!"

Mr. Stone retreated hastily to the yard, almost falling over George, who was curled up on the doorstep in the December sun.

"Scat, cat!" the old man shouted wrathfully.

"Let him be!" cried Mr. Leeds, who hitherto had never referred to George as anything but a pest. "I guess the beast has the right to take the air upon his own doorstep."

Sam turned away to hide a grin, but the things that Mr. Stone had said troubled him. Later that day he went across the lane to talk about them with Mr. Clay.

"Mr. Stone says our fortunes have fallen so low, the soldiers are refusing to re-enlist when their terms are up," he said gloomily. "How are we going to fight a war without an army? I wish I were old enough to enlist."

"The men have simply gone home for the

winter, but they'll be back when the fighting starts again in the spring," Mr. Clay declared. "It is true that the temporary dwindling of his forces has put General Washington in a bad spot, but he'll come back fighting. Some men show to best advantage when the odds are heaviest against them, and General Washington is such a man. So keep your courage up, Sam. This is no time for a good Patriot to be faint-hearted."

Sam squared his shoulders. "I won't let Mr. Stone's Tory talk get me down again," he promised.

And yet it bothered him that he was doing nothing to help his country. The closest he could get to the war was to listen to Tim Monroe brag about his adventures.

Now that the Congress was meeting in Baltimore, Tim acted as one of the relays in the chain of express riders carrying dispatches from Congress to General Washington in the American camp at McKonkey's Ferry on the bank of the Delaware. He could not resist swaggering a little before his friend, who never saw anything more exciting than the inside of the printshop.

One day in late December Mrs. Leeds opened the door of the shop and swept in on a blast of icy air. She waved an open letter at her husband.

"The post rider just brought this letter from my nephew, Joab. His company is with the army at McKonkey's Ferry. The poor boy writes that his clothes are in rags and that his feet are all but frozen because he does not have a pair of hose to his name."

"Tch, tch. I'm sorry about this. But there is nothing that we can do for him," the printer said.

Mrs. Leeds tossed her head indignantly. "I'll tell you what we can do! I have some woolen hose, as well as mufflers, caps, and mittens that I've been knitting for our soldiers. I want Sam to ride over to McKonkey's Ferry and take them to Joab. We couldn't give him a better Christmas present than warm feet."

Unable to believe in this unexpected stroke of luck, Sam glanced eagerly at Mr. Leeds. The printer scratched his chin thoughtfully. "I don't want Sam gallivanting about the country," he said at last. "There's plenty of work for him to do around here."

Sam sighed and returned to cutting paper. No adventure for him! Not even a piddling ride to McKonkey's Ferry that a five-year-old could make in safety.

But Mrs. Leeds was frowning. "If you won't

send Sam, you'll just have to go yourself, James Leeds. No nephew of mine is going to run naked in the snow while I have clothes to send him."

That settled it. The mere thought of the cold winds that blew across the Delaware gave Mr. Leeds a twinge of pain in his joints. He agreed that Sam should ride the shambling old mare Bessie, leaving home on the morning of December 24 and returning to Philadelphia on Christmas Day.

"And mind that you return promptly, with no loitering along the way," added Mr. Leeds, still disapproving of the whole thing.

Early on the morning of December 24, Sam carried his cat over to the Clay house. After George was settled comfortably before the kitchen fireplace, Ellen handed Sam two bulging saddlebags.

"Mama put up a little lunch for you."

Sam grinned as he hefted the saddlebags and compared them mentally to the meager bundle of bread and cheese that Mrs. Leeds had thrust into his pocket. "Your mother must have thought that she was making lunch for half-a-dozen boys."

Ellen had been holding one hand behind her back. Now she brought it out and held out a warm scarlet muffler and mittens. "I'll give them to you today, instead of on Christmas, because you'll need them on your ride."

Rather bashfully, Sam wound the muffler around his neck. He wasn't used to receiving gifts, but he looked so pleased that Ellen was satisfied. Then she was the one to be surprised as he thrust a small package, wrapped in paper from the printshop, into her hand.

"From George and me. If it snows, I may not get back in time to give it to you on Christmas."

Ellen unwrapped the paper eagerly and then dropped it as she stared in delight at what was cupped in her palm. It was the figure of a cat — of George — carved from applewood and smoothed and polished until it glowed with beauty.

"Ohh! How lovely."

Ellen had known that, like most boys, Sam was handy with a jackknife, but she hadn't been aware that he could do such exquisite work as this.

"Why, Sam, you're an artist!" She held the little wooden cat against her. "I'll cherish this."

"I'm glad you like it." His tone was rather gruff but happiness over her pleasure in his gift spilled out of his eyes to light his face. He pulled on his new mittens. "Thanks to you, my hands won't freeze on the ride to McKonkey's Ferry."

There was little travel on the road to McKonkey's Ferry that dismal December day. A few farmers were carting firewood to Philadelphia. An express rider passed Sam at a hard gallop. Then Sam passed a company of Pennsylvania Militia, trampling along the frozen road, some shouldering flintlock muskets, others armed with the long Pennsylvania rifles so much dreaded by the enemy.

At noon he munched the bread and cheese that lay handy in his pocket, saving the better fare in the saddlebags for supper. He wasn't sure how far he had come, but he thought that he must be nearing his destination. He was riding through a stand of thick woods when a Continental sentry stepped into the road and challenged him. Sam explained that he was taking some clothes to a soldier in the New York Artillery Company. Mrs. Leeds had told him that Joab Miller was the drummer boy in this company.

"The captain's name is Hamilton," he told the sentry.

At that the sentry nodded. "Ride on until you see an orchard near some farm buildings, about half a mile from the river. The artillery camp is in the orchard."

31

"Giddap, Bessie!" Sam cried, happy to be near the end of the long ride.

Bessie ambled on and soon Sam found himself in the midst of the main Continental camp.

Few of the men were wearing uniforms and those that Sam saw were worn and faded. A few were still in civilian clothes, others had on hunting shirts of deerskin or linsey-woolsey. Their shoes, that had tramped the long rough miles from the tip of Manhattan Island to the banks of the Delaware River, were tied together with rawhide or rags; some shoes were so broken that the bruised feet of the wearers left bloody marks upon the snow. Seeing them, Sam felt ashamed because he himself was wearing a pair of stout, whole brogans.

A few more questions directed him to a narrow farm lane that led to the orchard where the New York Artillery was camped. In the orchard, the winter twilight was lit by log fires blazing in front of a row of half-faced camps, built in the shelter of a stone wall. Everything about this little camp was snug and orderly. An alert sentry sent Sam to explain his presence to the captain, who had his quarters in an apple shed.

Sam tied Bessie at the door and knocked rather timidly. He could see a slim young officer in a faded blue uniform sitting on an up-ended keg at a rough plank table, writing in the company order book. The officer looked up at Sam's knock and fixed him with keen intelligent eyes.

"Captain Alexander Hamilton?" Sam asked.

The officer nodded and motioned Sam inside the shed. In spite of his shabby uniform and cracked boots, Captain Hamilton managed to look spruce and well-groomed. His hair was powdered and neatly clubbed, and the silver hilt of his sword gleamed in the candlelight.

"What brings you here?" he asked in a friendly voice. "You look young to be a recruit."

He dropped his quill pen and rubbed his cold hands together.

"I'm Sam Woodbury, sir, apprentice to Mr. Leeds, the Philadelphia printer. I came to — "

Sam's explanation was interrupted by a lean soldier, wearing the stripes of a sergeant on his threadbare sleeve, who stepped inside the shed and saluted.

"You wanted to see me, sir?"

"Orders from headquarters, Sergeant Drake," replied Captain Hamilton. "We are to cook enough rations for three days. Have you portioned out the beef that was brought in?"

"Yes, sir. The men have it in their cooking pots."

"Send a detail to the regimental bakers to draw three days' rations of bread." As the sergeant left the shed, Captain Hamilton turned back to Sam. "You were telling me what brought you to camp."

Sam explained about Joab's letter and the clothing that his aunt had sent him. The captain nodded. "Our horses are stabled in the barn up the lane; you'll probably find Miller there; he doubles as drummer and horse boy. He sleeps in the hayloft and you're welcome to share his quarters for the night, and to eat supper with our company. Fortunately we have something in the pot tonight and can offer hospitality."

Sam thanked him. He had been wondering, rather anxiously, where he was going to sleep that night.

As he was leading Bessie up the lane, his eyes caught the gleam of burnished metal reflecting the light of the campfires. Looking closer, he saw two brass cannon drawn off on one side of the lane. He stared at them eagerly, promising himself a closer look in the morning. For now, he wanted to find Joab Miller and get Bessie and himself settled for the night.

The big barn was lighted inside by lanterns hung on pegs along the wall. Besides some well-fed farm horses, there were a number of gun-teams in the stalls. As Sam stood wondering where he could put Bessie, a boy came in carrying two buckets of water. He wasn't much older than Sam, but he was taller, lean and sinewy and weather-burned. He was wearing a shabby blue uniform faced with red, and one knee of the breeches was ornamented by a clumsy patch. He eyed the strange boy with suspicion.

"Who are you? What are doing in here?"

"This is Colonel Woodbury's horse," Sam replied jauntily. "I'm supposed to stable it here."

The boy stared at Bessie, who certainly did not look like a battle charger. "Colonel Woodbury? Never heard of him. What's his regiment?"

"He's Commander of the Twelfth Legion," said Sam, who was very familiar with the Roman legions from his Latin studies.

"The Twelfth Leg — Oh! A wise fellow, eh? How would you like a punch in the nose?" the boy demanded, bristling.

"I'll give as good as I get," Sam growled, doubling his fists and glaring back.

But just then, Sergeant Drake walked into

the barn. Seeing that a fight was beginning, he roared at the boys, "None of that, you fellows. Miller, this boy rode into camp looking for you. Captain Hamilton sent him on here."

"Looking for me?" Joab Miller exclaimed. "I don't believe it! The way he talks, he could be a bedlamite* — or a spy."

"I'm as good a Patriot as you!" Sam said indignantly. "Your aunt, Mrs. Leeds, sent me from Philadelphia with some clothes for you. Just take the bundle off my saddle so I can stable my nag."

He didn't care where he slept that night as long as it wasn't near Joab Miller!

Joab's face had flushed an embarrassed scarlet. "Oh — I — I say — " he sputtered.

"Put your horse in the empty stall at the end of the line, boy," the sergeant told Sam. "Miller, take your bundle off the saddle and then go up to the loft to pitch down some hay for the nag."

"I'll take care of that myself," Sam said quickly.

He unsaddled Bessie, rubbed her down with a feed sack, fed and watered her. All this time Joab Miller was hanging around, speechless. When Sam stepped out of Bessie's stall with

* crazy person

his saddlebags over his arm, Joab was waiting for him. He wore a shamefaced look. He had bundled himself into Mr. Leeds' old watch-coat, in which Mrs. Leeds had rolled up the other garments, and when he saw that he had caught Sam's attention, he thrust out a foot in a shoe onto which the sole was bound with rawhide. Sam saw that he was wearing a pair of the heavy woolen hose his aunt had sent.

"They feel nice and warm," Joab muttered. "Thanks for riding over here with the clothes. I sure needed them. I found a fruitcake rolled up in the bundle. Let's divide it."

Sam's hard feelings disappeared in view of Joab's desire to be friendly. "Better hold off on the cake until later," he advised. "I heard Captain Hamilton say that there'll be boiled beef for supper. You're young to be a soldier," he added enviously.

"Most drummers are young. I'm from New Jersey, but I'm serving in a New York company because of my brother. He went to King's College, in New York, with Alex Hamilton. Alex organized this artillery company and got himself elected captain, so Jim joined up. And then I got Pa's permission to enlist as the company's drummer."

"Have you ever been in a battle?" Sam asked.

"Of course. The drummer always leads the company. I was in action on Long Island — White Plains — " Suddenly Joab turned away so Sam couldn't see his face. "Jim was killed at White Plains," he said in a low voice.

"That's hard luck," Sam faltered. "I'm sorry, Joab."

Joab drew a hard breath and turned back to Sam. "It was the fortunes of war." He abruptly changed the subject. "Let's go down to the camp and see about that beef you mentioned."

He stuffed half-a-dozen pairs of woolen hose into his pockets to distribute among his special friends in the company.

They found the men squatting in the doorways of their shelters, eating beef and turnip stew with iron spoons out of iron cups. Tony Mercer, another young private, had cooked Joab's rations with his own and he invited Sam to share the meal with them. He handed out small loaves of rubbery dark bread. All the soldiers were devouring this bread ravenously. Several of them told Sam that this was the best meal they had had in several weeks.

"I'll wager that the Hessians, yonder in Trenton, are having a grand feast tonight. Germans set great store by the Christmas Eve feast," one man remarked. He scraped his cup for the last drop of stew. "Their favorite food is roast goose with onion stuffing. Or suckling pig roasted with an apple in its mouth, and potatoes basted with hot fat until they're covered with a crispy brown crust. Then they have a cake called 'kuchen.' It's made of apples baked in a rich crust with sugar and cinnamon and thick cream poured over — "

"Stop!" Joab groaned. "You're killing me."

The mention of cake made him remember the fruitcake his aunt had sent him. He unwrapped it and cut it into as many small pieces as possible, to share among his friends. Until now, Sam had forgotten the contents of the bulging saddlebags that Ellen had given him. He unbuckled them hastily. "I guess there'll be some holiday fixings in here," he told his companions.

He pulled out half-a-dozen man-sized chicken and ham sandwiches wrapped in a linen napkin. There were also mincemeat turnovers, two huge squares of gingerbread, and a dozen rich sugar cookies. Sam divided the food among the three of them in Tony's shelter and the men in the shelters on each side. While they ate, Joab and Tony discussed the movement of troops that had taken place that day.

"The General must be expecting a battle," Tony declared. "Why else would he be concentrating the whole army here at McKonkey's Ferry?"

"Do you expect the British to cross the river?" Sam asked in surprise.

"Not them!" said Joab with a laugh. "General Washington brought all the boats on the river over to this side and the lobsterbacks haven't sprouted wings yet!"

"It will be *this* army that will cross the Delaware," someone else said.

"Through all that ice?" Sam asked incredulously.

"Oh, a little thing like flood water or grinding ice won't stop General Washington, if he makes up his mind to cross."

Later, Joab and Sam made their bed in the sweet-scented hay in the barn loft. They spread Joab's blanket over them, and the heat from the animals in the stalls below helped to keep them warm. Joab talked on and on about his wartime experiences.

"There's no more important post in the army than that of drummer," he declared. "We tap Reveille at dawn to get the men out of their blankets. We set the pace when the troops are on the march, and we're the ones who have to be on the alert to beat To Arms, in case of an enemy attack."

Sam found all this vastly interesting, but he

was very tired and soon his head began to nod. The last thing he heard before he fell asleep was Joab's tongue wagging away. Then suddenly it was daybreak. Sam was alone in the hay and Joab was down in the orchard vigorously beating Reveille on his drum.

Sam Hears the Roar
of Cannon

"IT'S Christmas Day," Sam said remembering.

Dark clouds heavy with snow were scudding across the sky. Sam shivered as he thought of the long cold ride back to Philadelphia. He pulled on his shoes and descended the hayloft ladder.

A stocky man in homespun and sturdy boots was watering the farm horses. Sam asked if he might borrow a pail to bring water from the pump for Bessie.

"I haven't seen you before," the farmer said. "New recruit?"

"No, sir. I'm from Philadelphia. I brought some clothes to Joab Miller. I'm starting home this morning."

As he spoke, Sam wondered rather hopelessly what his chances were for getting some breakfast before taking to the road. Joab had disappeared and he didn't want to go prowling around the camp by himself. Suddenly his problem was solved.

"If you're not in a hurry," the farmer said, "my wife would appreciate some help in the kitchen. General Knox and some other officers are quartered at our house. My wife is a red-hot Patriot, and this being Christmas Day, she's bound to give them a good breakfast, even if we ourselves don't eat for the rest of the winter. But our hired girl is sick and Mrs. Bixby is beside herself with all the work."

"I'll help," Sam replied promptly.

"Good! Go along and tell Mrs. Bixby that I sent you. I'll look after your horse."

Mrs. Bixby gave Sam a delighted welcome. The farmhouse kitchen was warm from the heat of the huge fireplace. Sausages gave off a delicious odor as they sputtered in an iron spider, and a great kettle of cornmeal mush was simmering and steaming on the crane.

As soon as the officers had finished their breakfast, Mrs. Bixby fried some cakes for Sam. The sausages were all gone, but she fried a slice of home-cured ham for him to eat with his eggs. Afterward, Sam cleared the dining table and offered to wash the huge stack of dishes. When he had finished scouring the spider*, he carried in two buckets of water

* black iron skillet with legs

from the pump in the yard and several arm-loads of wood from the shed.

"You're a good boy, Sam," Mrs. Bixby said, when he was ready to go. She handed him a bundle containing a loaf of bread, some thick slices of ham, and some caraway cookies to eat on the road to Philadelphia. Sam thanked her and walked back down the lane to the orchard. He hoped to find Joab to say good-bye before he started home.

In the orchard, it was plain to see that the New York Artillery Company was making ready to break camp. The men were drawn up for inspection by their keen-eyed young captain. Joab stood stiffly with his drumsticks poised above his drum. While Sam watched from the other side of the stone wall, the artillery horses were led out of the barn and harnessed to the brass cannon and the ammunition carts.

Captain Hamilton shouted an order and the New York Artillery swung smartly down the lane and turned into the road, Joab marching ahead and beating a stirring tattoo upon his drum. Captain Hamilton strode beside one of his cannon and from time to time he patted the gleaming barrel fondly, as if he knew that it was a friend on which he could depend.

"Good-bye Joab! Good luck!" Sam shouted.

Joab did not turn his head, and completely forgetful of Mr. Leeds' order that he return to Philadelphia without delay this Christmas morning, Sam jumped off the wall and fell in at the rear of the marching company. Because there were so few uniforms in this army, no one questioned a boy whose clothes were as shabby as those worn by most of the soldiers. So Sam tagged along, determined to speak to Joab before he left. It wouldn't be sensible to wish his new friend a Merry Christmas under these circumstances, but at least he could wish him good luck in whatever enterprise lay ahead for the little army.

Upon reaching the river, Captain Hamilton ordered the cannon parked beside the rest of the Continental artillery, close to where the wooden ferry dock jutted out into the wind-tossed, ice-choked river. There were only twenty pieces in all, cannon of all types and sizes. A few had been captured from the enemy and were in fairly good shape, but most of the cannon were ancient, battered relics of the French and Indian War, many of them pitted with rust.

More troops kept arriving at the ferry all afternoon. The soldiers built fires of fence rails and logs wherever a stone fence or a stand of trees offered some protection from the raw cold wind. Boats were drawn up on the riverbank at every point where the condition of the ice made embarkation possible.

Sam wandered through the artillery park until he found Joab crouched down in the poor shelter of a cannon with his blanket draped around his shoulders.

"I thought that you had started for home hours ago," he said when he saw Sam.

"I wanted to wish you luck in the battle." Sam untied the bundle of lunch that Mrs. Bixby had given him and sat down beside Joab. Joab shared half his blanket with Sam and they munched bread and ham while they watched some soldiers working with axes and picks to clear away the ice that had jammed against the dock.

"The regiment of Marblehead fishermen are in charge of the boats," Joab said. "General Washington always calls on them when the army has to be transported anywhere by boat."

Sam stared wordlessly at the turbulent river where huge cakes of ice were grinding together with a sinister sound. It didn't seem possible that an army with cannon and horses could be ferried across that wild water in small boats.

Some of the Massachusetts fishermen were

poling hay barges into position at the end of the dock.

"We'll embark the cannon out there where the water is deep," Joab explained.

A group of officers came out of the ferry house and walked briskly out on the dock, their dark cloaks flapping in the wind. One, who walked with the free stride of an athlete, stood taller than the others. With a thrill, Sam recognized General Washington.

The last time he had seen the General was on the day in 1775 when Washington had ridden out of Philadelphia on his way to Massachusetts to take command of the Continental Army. Sam felt a lump swell his throat as he and Joab jumped up and joined in the cheers with which the soldiers greeted their general.

Later, the boys heard General Knox talking to Captain Hamilton in the dusk.

"The General plans to attack the Hessians in Trenton at dawn. Stand ready to get your cannon aboard as soon as the fishermen lay the barges alongside the dock. The watchword tonight is 'Liberty or Death'!"

As soon as it was dark, the soldiers marched down to the riverbank and began to clamber into the boats. These were black-painted, flat-bottomed canoe-shaped boats that had been made to carry cargo on the river. Each held about thirty-five men and had four or six oarsmen. Every soldier was armed with a musket or rifle, a bayonet, sword, or tomahawk. Each carried a cartridge box containing ammunition and flints, a rolled blanket, and a haversack packed with rations.

The wind had risen to a howling gale and the air was full of swirling snowflakes. General Knox stood on the dock, roaring out orders for the embarkation of his precious artillery. Sometimes he would grab the bridle of a nervous horse and drag it aboard a barge by sheer strength. If a cannon bogged down in the slushy mud at the end of the dock, there was General Knox with his broad shoulder against the wheel, helping his straining men to push it to safety.

It was quite dark now and snowing heavily. Up and down the riverbank cargo boats were being launched with much shouting and shoving. The New York Artillery moved up on the dock and Sam trailed along, unwilling to say good-bye to Joab. No one noticed him, but somehow in the darkness, the crush of people, and the falling snow, he and Joab became separated. Realizing suddenly that he had no right to be on the dock, Sam tried to shove through the crowd to the riverbank. He was jostled this way and that and almost pushed into the river as men dragged a cannon toward the barge. Then a big hand fell on his shoulder and he found himself being propelled rapidly back toward the barge.

"This way!" General Knox shouted in his ear. "Step lively! You're holding up the whole regiment."

He gave Sam a push that landed him on his face on the snow-carpeted barge. As he struggled to his feet the barge was pushed out into the water and the oarsmen in the galley ahead began to row. Barge and galley crept out into the full force of the cutting wind, which drove snow into the faces of the men and down their necks, and drenched them with the freezing water that washed into the barge. The shore disappeared and the world became a flood of black water filled with grinding ice, and a screaming sleet-laden wind.

Sam knelt down beside one of the cannon and held his mittened hands before his numb face. He could not see Joab, but he knew that he was somewhere near. He thought of Ellen and Tim and pictured their astonishment if they could see him cruising across the Delaware to do battle with the Hessians.

After two hours of battling wind and current, the barge nosed in at the ferry dock on the New Jersey side of the river. Sam rose stiffly to his feet and peered toward the shore. Now that fate had brought him this far, he was determined to stick with his friends of the New York Artillery and finish the adventure.

General Washington and General Knox had crossed in one of the cargo boats. Now the Commander in Chief sat on his big horse and gave commands in a ringing voice which was echoed by Knox's deep-chested roar. The cannon began to move along the icy dock.

Sam found himself helping to push an ammunition cart. "I really am part of the army!" he thought in astonishment.

Behind him, someone was leading a horse. Dimly seen through the snow, this soldier looked a trifle shorter than some of the others. Sam was sure that it was Joab. He waited until they reached the bank and then twitched the other boy's sleeve. "Hello, Joab," he whispered.

Joab jumped. "Sam! Great guns! What are you doing here?"

"Colonel Woodbury is off to the wars," Sam muttered.

Joab smothered a laugh. "Stay close to me," he whispered. "They may not discover you in the darkness."

After harnessing Joab's horse to Sam's ammunition cart, they found shelter against a stone wall. Joab kept thumping his arms across his chest. "It's getting colder every minute! Why don't we get started before we freeze solid?"

But they had to wait until the entire army had crossed over into New Jersey. No fires were permitted because General Washington planned to surprise the enemy at dawn. Two men froze to death before the march on Trenton finally started.

Sam dared not stay near the head of the company with Joab, but trudged along in his old place behind the ammunition cart. It was nine miles to Trenton. General Sullivan was leading half the army along the lower river road, while General Washington and the rest of the troops took a higher road. At dawn the two divisions were supposed to catch the enemy in a cross fire from different ends of the town.

The New York Artillery marched with Washington. The wheels of the cannon had been bound with rags to muffle noise. The deeply rutted road was glazed with ice and the men slipped and struggled as they stumbled along, heads down, clutching their muskets with numbed fingers. Their feet left bloody marks where the sharp edges of the ice cut through their worn shoes. Sam gave the muffler Ellen had made to a soldier who had no hat, and the man tied it gratefully over his head. Sam knew that Ellen would understand when he told her what had happened to her Christmas present.

Halfway to Trenton, the officers called a halt for rest and food. The men pulled black bread and cold pork from their haversacks and made a hasty breakfast. Sam gnawed hungrily on a crust of bread he had saved.

"Fall in!" came Captain Hamilton's low command.

"Press on, boys, press on!" It was General Washington riding back along the column. He held a piece of black bread in his hand and chewed on it as he rode along.

The weary column slopped forward through icy slush that was now ankle deep. Captain Hamilton dropped back to say something to the driver of the ammunition cart, then to Sam's dismay, the captain fell into step beside him.

"I thought I left you up ahead, Miller," he said, mistaking Sam for Joab.

There was a heavy pause. Sam knew that he had been discovered. He wondered desperately what the captain would do to him.

Captain Hamilton moved closer and peered

at him through the gloom. "Is that you, Miller? No! By Jove, you're not Miller —"

"I'm Sam Woodbury," Sam stammered.

The captain was so astonished that he slipped into a rut and would have fallen if Sam hadn't grabbed his arm. "What are you doing here?" he demanded, when he had regained his balance. "Don't you know that there's going to be a battle?"

"Give me a gun!" Sam begged him. "I'll do my part! Not that I had any intention of crossing the river, sir. I only meant to say good-bye to Joab. But in the darkness General Knox mistook me for a soldier and pushed me onto the barge."

Captain Hamilton gave a muffled laugh. "Well, I can see that you had small chance of resisting the general. But now I don't know what to do with you. General Washington would be furious if he knew that we had a noncombatant, and a boy at that, in the company. Well, stay to the rear. I'll send you back at the first opportunity."

Spies had reported to General Washington that the Hessians had spent Christmas Eve and Christmas Day in feasting, drinking, and carousing, and now most of them were in a sodden sleep. This was good news for the Americans. But it was bad news when an officer reported that some of the men had not kept their guns dry in the storm.

"Push on and charge with the bayonet!" Washington ordered.

In the dreary light of the winter dawn they crept up to the town with its quiet, deserted streets. Suddenly a crackle of musketry sounded from over near Assunpunk Creek. General Sullivan was going into action!

The sound of gunfire aroused the Hessians and they came pouring out into the streets, a confused mass of soldiers in yellow and blue uniforms, wearing tall brass-fronted caps and fiercely waxed mustaches. They milled about aimlessly while American marksmen picked them off. Finally officers burst out of the houses and rushed among the men, beating at them with the flats of their swords and shouting orders in German. Soon the Hessians had formed into orderly companies and were firing back at the Americans.

Captain Hamilton and the other artillery officers had swung their cannon into position where they could rake the main street of Trenton with grapeshot. Joab beat the Attack upon his drum and the spirited tattoo was caught up by the other Continental drummers. They were answered by an ominous roll from the Hessian kettle drums and a silver call from the trumpets of a company of British Light Horse that came riding to the aid of the Hessians.

Under the American bombardment, the Hessians rolled two of their cannon into position and opened fire. They had fired only two rounds when Sam, looking down from the top of King Street, saw a company of American riflemen peppering away at the enemy from behind trees and fences. Other Continentals swarmed forward, right over the Hessian cannon, yelling and using bayonets or clubbing with rifles and muskets to subdue the foe. The Hessians retreated, and the Continentals seized the big cannons and toppled them into the ditch at the side of the road.

Colonel Rahl, the Hessian Commander, came rushing out of the house where he had been sleeping off the effects of yesterday's feast. An aide ran up, leading his battle charger, and the colonel made a flying mount. He galloped along the quivering line of Hessian infantry and British Light Horse. "Forward!" he shouted, waving his sword toward the Americans.

His men surged after him up King Street, pouring a hot but poorly directed fire into the Americans. To Sam, it seemed as if every man in the Hessian ranks was firing directly at him. Stark terror turned his legs to jelly, but then he saw Joab to the front and one side of the line of American cannon, still staunchly beating his drum. Sam felt disgusted with his own cowardice. He was looking wildly around for a weapon when one of the gunners shouted at him.

"You, boy! More grape!"

Sam dashed to fetch grapeshot from the cart. He stood by while the cannoneers swabbed out the bore of the cannon, poured in powder, rammed in shot, and held a match ready.

"Fire!" shouted Captain Hamilton.

The two brass cannon roared, belching fire and smoke, spraying the street with grapeshot. With a feeling of sick horror, Sam saw Hessians topple over like toy soldiers, some to lie still in the slush, others to drag themselves painfully to the rear of their lines. So this was war! It was a good thing that a fellow had little time to think.

The British horsemen were galloping away to escape by the bridge over Assunpunk Creek. The Hessians closed their ranks and gave the Continentals another volley of musketry.

Sam felt a hot, stinging pain. "Ouch!" he yelled, as he grabbed at his side. Then he forgot his own pain as he saw Joab crumple to the ground. Ignoring the bullets that were zinging around him, he darted to where his friend was sprawled in the slush.

Joab's hat had fallen off and a trickle of blood was oozing from a gash on his head and running down his forehead and cheek. Sam pulled the drum from around his friend's neck and slung it over his own arm. Then he took hold of Joab's shoulders and dragged him back to the ammunition cart. The exertion made his own wound throb and he was breathing in gasps by the time he had succeeded in pulling and pushing Joab into the almost-empty cart. He covered him with one of the blankets that had been left there during the battle.

The Continentals had charged the Hessians and a bitter hand-to-hand struggle was going on in the street. Someone shouted that Colonel Rahl had been fatally wounded. At that the Hessians lifted their helmets on their gun barrels as a sign that they surrendered.

Sam was only dimly conscious of what was going on during the last minutes of the battle. He had wet his grimy handkerchief in a puddle and was try to stop the flow of blood coming from the wound in Joab's scalp. Joab lay so still and white that Sam wondered, in dread, if he could be dying.

After the cannon fell silent, Sergeant Drake

called to a soldier who had been a barber-surgeon before the war, and thus had enough medical knowledge to make him the company doctor. The soldier climbed into the cart to examine Joab.

"It's not a fatal wound," he pronounced. Sam sent up a prayer of thankfulness.

From his doctor's bag, the soldier took a pair of shears with which he cut away the blood-matted hair around Joab's wound. Next, he washed the wound with the contents of a flask of spirits. The stinging pain of this caused Joab to open his eyes and give a low moan.

Sam had pulled off his jacket and was tearing his calico shirt into strips. "It's a good thing that some of us still have shirts," the barber said with a grin as he bandaged Joab's head. "They come in handy at a time like this."

He covered Joab with the blanket and jumped out of the cart. Sam, who was buttoning himself into his jacket, bit his lip to hold back a groan as a burning pain seared across his ribs. He had been so concerned about Joab that he had forgotten his own wound.

"What ails you?" the barber demanded.

"I — I guess I was hit too," Sam muttered.

"Off with that jacket! Let's have a look at you."

The bullet had passed between Sam's arm and body, tearing his jacket and raising a burning red welt along his ribs. The barber whistled. "Lucky for you that it wasn't a smidgin closer."

He reached under the cart for the pail of axle grease. He smeared grease thickly on the wound and bandaged it with the last of Sam's shirt. "You'll be stiff and sore for a few days," he told Sam cheerfully. He hurried away to aid another wounded man.

Incredible as it seemed, no Americans had been killed in the battle and only a few had been wounded.

In the town, some Patriot women had hastily set up soup kitchens and were feeding the cold, hungry Continentals. Captain Hamilton dismissed his company so that the men could get some food. Sergeant Drake mounted guard over the battery.

"If you see to it that Joab stays covered up, I'll walk down there and get us some soup," Sam offered.

The sergeant nodded. "Go along. But hurry! When General Washington gives the word, this army is going to move fast. We've got to get back across the river before Lord Cornwallis can catch us with the main British Army."

Sam moved stiffly off down King Street, carrying two pails in which to fetch the soup. The battle had made a shambles of this part of the pretty town. As Sam picked his way through the mess and litter, he decided that seeing war at close quarters robbed it of all its romance.

He joined a queue of soldiers in front of a house where two women had set a great kettle of steaming hot soup on the stone doorstep. Sam presented the pails he was carrying. "This is for three men," he explained.

One of the women stared at him. "Surely you are too young to be a soldier!" she exclaimed.

"I just happened to be along," Sam told her. An appealing smile lighted his thin face under his battered hat. "My friend, a drummer boy, was wounded in the battle."

"Wait here," the woman said. She hurried into the house and when she came back she handed Sam a warm loaf of bread wrapped in a napkin. Her companion filled his pails brimming with rich soup. "Don't get into any more battles until you're grown up," the bread woman advised, sending Sam on his way with a friendly pat.

Gritting his teeth because of the soreness of his wound, Sam hurried back to his friends.

Just as he reached the cart, a trumpet blew in the village.

"That means that we march in half an hour," said Sergeant Drake.

"Here's your dinner," Sam panted, handing him a pail of soup and half the crusty new-baked loaf. "How's Joab?"

"He's awake and he asked for you."

Sam clambered into the cart. Joab's eyes, fever-bright, peered at him over the edge of the blanket. "Well, Colonel Woodbury," he croaked. "We both came through the battle."

"And we won a great victory. I heard in the town that we captured a thousand prisoners and a lot of supplies."

Sam knelt beside his friend and slipped an arm around his shoulders to support him while he sipped soup from a cup. When Joab had eaten his fill, Sam eased him down carefully and then sat beside him in the cart while he ate his own dinner. Soon Joab fell asleep. His face was pale beneath the bandage, but Sam had the thankful feeling that he was going to be all right.

When the army began its march back to the ferry, the way seemed twice as long as it had been in the pre-dawn hours before the battle. The men had won a precious victory for their country but now the excitement was over, and they could feel how cold and weary they really were.

As Sam trudged along, he felt it was only the burning of his wound that kept him from tumbling into a nice soft snowdrift and falling asleep. In the cart, Joab bore the bumping and lurching bravely, and at last they came to the ferry on the New Jersey side of the river.

Sam watched a group of prisoners being herded down to the boats by rangy American riflemen in buckskin shirts. For all their fierce mustaches, the Hessians looked lost and bewildered. Sam was surprised to discover that he felt sorry for them. After all, they hadn't left their homeland of their own free will, but had been sold into foreign service by their prince, at so much a head, as if they were cattle.

"But at least they're about to find out that one tale they've heard about Americans isn't true," Sam thought with a tired grin.

A warning had been spread among the Hessian regiments by the British that any Hessian who permitted himself to be taken prisoner by the Continentals would certainly be cooked and eaten by his captors!

Back at the camp in the Bixby orchard, Joab insisted that he wanted to return to his old warm quarters in the hay. With Sam's help, he climbed the ladder to the loft and soon both boys were in an exhausted sleep.

It was bright morning outside when Sam awoke in the dim hayloft. Joab was still asleep. Moving softly so as not to wake him, Sam crawled stiffly from beneath the covers. Pain burned along his side as he made his way down the ladder and to Bessie's stall. Bessie greeted him with a friendly nicker. She looked well cared for, so Sam knew that Mr. Bixby had looked after her in his absence.

"It's back to Philadelphia for us today," he told her with a sigh.

Before he could get the mare saddled, Mr. Bixby came into the barn. The farmer was excited over the news of the battle that he had received from returning soldiers. He insisted upon Sam going up to the farmhouse with him, and there, while Mrs. Bixby served him a hearty breakfast, Sam gave them a firsthand account of the victory at Trenton. He also told Mrs. Bixby about Joab's wound, and the warmhearted woman declared she would get Captain Hamilton's permission to move Joab up to the farmhouse until he was fully recovered.

The Enemy Moves In

THE printshop was dark when Sam rode into the Leeds' yard that evening. He took Bessie to her stall in the shed, fed her, brought her water, and covered her with a blanket.

"I guess you're glad to be home again," he said, slapping her rump as he left the stall.

For himself, he couldn't feel any gladness. A vision of the cane Mr. Leeds kept behind the kitchen door taunted him as he tramped the path to the house. Evidently the creaking of the pump had alerted the printer to the return of his apprentice; he was waiting when Sam rapped at the door. He jerked the door open and scowled at the boy standing cold and tired in the winter starlight.

"So you finally decided to come home!" He reached out and fastened a hand in the front of Sam's jacket. "Where have you been, you worthless vagabond?" he demanded, as he pulled the boy in the kitchen.

Mrs. Leeds jumped up from her chair before the fire and slammed the door against the cold.

"I told you to come straight home after delivering Mrs. Leeds' bundle to Joab!" Mr. Leeds scolded.

He fetched Sam a clout on the ear that sent him staggering back against the door.

"I've been to McKonkey's Ferry," Sam gasped. "And to Trenton in New Jersey — "

"Trenton? A likely story. What took you there?"

"What about the clothes I sent to Joab?" Mrs. Leeds put in. "Probably poor Joab never saw them."

"He did too," Sam protested. "Ouch!" he yelled, as Mr. Leeds grabbed the cane from behind the door and began to switch his legs.

"I'll beat a sense of duty and responsibility into you if I have to wear out your hide doing it," Mr. Leeds said grimly.

After that one outburst, Sam took his punishment in silence, although he capered about, trying to dodge his master's blows. His wound had throbbed all during the long ride from McKonkey's Ferry and now it hurt unbearably, but he'd die, he vowed, before he told Mr. Leeds about it. At last Mr. Leeds let his switching arm fall to his side. "Now, Sam, give us the truth," he said.

Before Sam could speak, the outside door opened and Mr. Clay walked into the kitchen. "I've been knocking in vain," he exclaimed. His pleasant face lighted up when he saw Sam. "So here you are, safe home. We were worried about you." His eyes clouded as he noted Sam's pale face and mouth clamped tight with pain. Mr. Clay's eyes shifted to the cane in Mr. Leeds' hand. " 'Tis a warm welcome you give the boy," he said sternly.

"A welcome to teach him his duty," Mr. Leeds snapped. He threw the cane into the corner. "The rascal claims that he has been to Trenton."

"So I have," Sam insisted.

"Across the river to the Hessian camp?" Mr. Leeds tapped the floor impatiently with his foot. "Come now, Sam, you'd better give us the truth of where you really have been and what mischief you've been up to."

"Why don't we listen to what the boy has to tell us?" Mr. Clay suggested.

Sam, sullen from the treatment that he had received, was tempted not to tell Mr. Leeds about the battle, but he realized that by now General Washington's express to Congress would have ridden through the city and soon the victory would be common news.

"There's been a battle and I was in it!" he burst out. "General Washington crossed the Delaware on Christmas night and surprised the Hessians at Trenton."

Once he had launched upon his tale, the words tumbled out in a flood. "Captain Hamilton — Joab — General Washington — the ice-choked river — the battle on King Street — "

Mrs. Leeds and the two men listened in growing astonishment and excitement. "I can't believe that the boy has actually been through all this," Mr. Leeds muttered.

"Nonsense!" Mr. Clay said sharply. "How could he invent such things? There has been a battle and our Sam has been in it." He thumped Sam's shoulder. "Wait until Ellen hears about this! But what's the matter, Sam?"

Sam had clutched a chair for support. Suddenly the room was whirling around him in a haze of pain and weariness. "I — guess it's my wound," he whispered.

"Wound?" cried Mr. Leeds. "You said naught about having been wounded."

His hands were surprisingly gentle as he helped Sam off with his jacket and unwound the bandage from around his ribs.

"Where is your shirt?" Mrs. Leeds demanded, as her husband made Sam sit down.

"The Doc used it to make a bandage for

Joab's head wound," said Sam, shamefaced at his own weakness.

Mr. Clay was peering at the angry-looking welt on Sam's side. "Well, Leeds, now perhaps you are sorry that you were so handy with that cane!"

Mr. Leeds nodded silently. He looked deeply troubled. He believed in flogging for boys as a means of discipline, but at heart he was not a cruel man.

Mrs. Leeds had taken the kettle from the fireplace crane and was pouring hot water into a basin. With hands more gentle than Sam could have dreamed that hers could be, she washed the wound and then applied some herbal healing salve. By the time she had bound on a fresh bandage of soft linen, Sam was alternately shivering with chills or burning with fever. Mr. Leeds made him drink some hot soup, and then they put him to bed in the quilts they had spread on the fireside settle. They even allowed George to come in and see him. The cat leaped up on the settle, purring his happiness over the return of his friend.

"George, old boy," Sam murmured sleepily. His fingers dug into the cat's thick copper-bright fur. George's purr became a rumble. He curled up at Sam's feet and his claws kneaded at the quilt in vast contentment. Surprisingly, Mrs. Leeds did not protest.

Sam was grateful for this change in the attitude of his master and his wife, but he was so tired! And they kept on asking so many questions about Joab and the battle that he wished he could steal away with George to his cold, quiet bed in the loft above the printshop.

Early the next morning, Sam's news about the battle was announced officially by the Town Criers of Philadelphia. And even more thrilling news about another victory was brought by an express rider from Washington's headquarters a few days later.

After allowing his exhausted soldiers three days of rest after Trenton, General Washington had whipped back across the Delaware to New Jersey to attack the main British Army under Lord Cornwallis. Moving his little force with shrewd and brilliant strategy, Washington proved that he was more than a match for the slow British generals. He defeated the British Army in a hard fight at Princeton and captured a baggage train loaded with supplies that the Continentals needed badly. Then, having sent the King's soldiers back to New York, smarting from this major defeat, Washington and his men went into winter quarters at Morristown, New Jersey.

Sam thought often of Joab Miller and wondered how he was. Weeks passed and then one day in February a postrider stopped at the Leeds' house with two letters. One was for Mrs. Leeds from her brother. It told that Joab had received an honorable discharge from the army and that he had been invalided home to the New Jersey farm. The other letter was for Sam from Joab. Joab wrote that he was almost recovered from his wound, and that come spring, he intended to enlist in a New Jersey company. He also wrote that Captain Hamilton had been promoted to the rank of Colonel and was now serving as an aide-de-camp to General Washington.

"Will I ever see them all again?" Sam wondered, as he worked at the unexciting tasks of washing type, mixing ink, and running errands.

In the spring of 1777, General Howe decided to make another attempt to capture Philadelphia. This time he would make use of the strong British fleet and approach the city by water.

But it was July before General Washington's spies informed him that the British fleet had set sail from New York. Anxious weeks followed. No one knew exactly where General Howe would land his troops.

Because of the unsettled state of affairs, business came almost to a standstill in Philadelphia. For the first time since Sam had been at the printshop, work was slow. Every morning Mr. Leeds would send him over to the State House to see if there was any news of the army. Finally, one morning late in August, Sam came pelting home wild with excitement.

"The British have landed at the head of Chesapeake Bay!" he panted, as he burst into the printshop.

Mr. Leeds pushed back his chair from his desk. A worried frown creased his forehead. The enemy was headed for Philadelphia, and if General Howe captured the town, he, James Leeds, would meet with harsh treatment, perhaps death. It was well known that he was one of the leading Patriot printers who had printed material of a highly treasonable nature in the eyes of the King's supporters.

"What news of our army?" he demanded.

Sam wiped his dripping face with the sleeve of his shirt. "An express from General Washington has informed the Congress that the army will pass through Philadelphia this afternoon on its way to meet the British. There's going to be a big battle, sir!"

"Yes, Sam," the printer said soberly. "And upon this battle will rest the fate of Philadelphia." For the moment, he and Sam did not

71

seem to be master and apprentice but only two Americans talking man to man.

"Do you think we'll win?" Sam asked eagerly.

"General Washington is a magnificent soldier. Given the right army, he could lick the breeches off any British general in the world."

"Our soldiers are a brave lot of fellows," Sam said, remembering Trenton.

"They're brave enough, and their hearts are in what they're fighting for. It's the equipment and the training that they lack. The British Army moves like a machine, and it has the traditions of centuries of soldiering behind it. But Washington has been struggling for two years to form the raw militia of the thirteen states into a national army. They say that he worked wonders during the winter at Morristown, but — "

"It will be something to see our army parade through Philadelphia," Sam said wistfully.

Mr. Leeds gave him an understanding glance. "I suppose that every boy in town will be posted somewhere along the route to see our men go by. Well, you may go too, Sam. There's no work to be done today."

Sam could hardly believe his luck. He wondered if he would see Joab Miller with the troops. Joab must have re-enlisted by this time.

Sam was just putting on a clean shirt when he heard Tim Monroe shouting from the street below. "Sam! I say, Sam!"

Sam put his head out of the loft window. Tim waved at him from Chief's back. "Aren't you going to see the troops?"

"Yep. I've got the rest of the day off."

"Come on, then. Chief can carry us both."

Sam tore down the ladder and a few moments later he was riding behind Tim as Chief trotted out Chestnut Street beyond Seventh, where the town fell behind and farms and woods began.

"Here's a good place." Tim rode off the road and tethered Chief in a grassy spot behind a little knoll. "We couldn't find a better place from which to review the troops, Colonel Woodbury," Tim said as the boys threw themselves down on the knoll. They peered along the road, eager for the first appearance of the Continentals. Then suddenly Sam's ears caught the beat of drums and the thud of many hooves. "Here they come!" he cried, as some horsemen appeared around a bend in the road.

It was the Continental Light Horse, four regiments strong, a gallant company. Some of the horsemen wore green coats; others wore blue faced with red. The sun sparkled on their helmets plumed with horse hair. They rode past the knoll with a creaking of saddle leather and a rattling of sabres. As one troop drew near, the trumpeter lifted his silver bugle and sent a clear trill of notes mounting on the summer air. Sam's heart swelled with pride.

"I'll wager that the King has no finer horse troops than ours," he said stoutly.

But before the long parade of Continental troops had passed, the boys realized that the riders of the Light Horse regiments were by far the best-looking units in the army. This was because most of the horsemen were wealthy men who provided their own mounts, arms, and uniforms. The four divisions of infantry that followed the horse troops looked little better than the ragged troops that Sam had seen at McKonkey's Ferry.

Only a few companies wore the official blue and buff of the Continental Army. Most of the lean and rangy soldiers were dressed in linen hunting shirts dyed a butternut brown. Some shouldered flintlock muskets, some long rifles, a few had shotguns. Good guns were scarce, but the bronzed hands that carried them were sinewy and determined. The most important result of the bitter campaign of the year before was that the hardships the men had

74

endured together had welded Washington's mixed troops into a real army.

Suddenly Sam saw Joab trudging along between a tall fifer and another drummer. Although he looked hot and tired, he was steadfastly beating the rhythm of the march for the men of the New Jersey company.

"Joab!" Sam yelled. "Joab!"

He ran into the road and fell into step with the little drum corps. Joab grinned at him, then stopped beating and edged over to shake hands.

"Good luck, Joab!" Sam shouted, as his friend ran back to his place and caught up the beat again. "If you return through Philadelphia, try to come to Sassafras Lane."

"I'll come —" Joab's voice came trailing back as the regiment marched on.

A lump rose in Sam's throat as he stood at the side of the road and watched Joab march away. Joab was going into battle. It could be that he would never come back to look for Sam in Sassafras Lane.

Several days later, General Washington's army met the enemy along Brandywine Creek. The superior numbers and organization of the British troops told heavily in the struggle that followed. The Americans were defeated, and now the road to Philadelphia was open to the British.

Express riders carried the bad news to Congress and soon the Town Criers were ringing their bells and proclaiming the defeat of the Continental Army at Brandywine. The Congress quickly packed up the state papers and fled to the town of York. Tories came out into the open to taunt the despondent Patriots.

In Sassafras Lane, Sam and Mr. Leeds worked far into the night, dismantling the press and loading it and the fonts of type into a cart. This done, Sam helped Mrs. Leeds pack clothes and household treasures. Mr. Leeds dared not let the British catch him in Philadelphia, so he planned to follow the Congress to York, where he could continue his government work. He and Mrs. Leeds would live with their married daughter, and he would set up his printing press in her barn. There was no room for Sam in that crowded household, so Mr. Clay had offered to give Sam a home until his master could return to Philadelphia.

"Sam will more than earn his keep by helping me in the bookshop," Mr. Clay said.

"Then you plan to keep the shop open?" returned Mr. Leeds.

" 'Tis the best thing to do under the circumstances."

A glance of understanding passed between the two Patriots, then Mr. Leeds nodded gravely. "It's true that they have naught against you, but it would mean prison or a rope's end for me, if they captured me."

"That's true," Mr. Clay agreed. "But as far as the British know, I have always been neutral."

Sam, who was standing near, looked at him in amazement.

"Thomas Stone knows that you are a Patriot," Mr. Leeds warned.

The bookseller shrugged off any idea of a threat from old Mr. Stone. "Don't worry about me."

This conversation troubled Sam deeply. He hated to think of Mr. Clay posing as a neutral and being friendly to the enemy just to keep his shop open.

Mr. and Mrs. Leeds started for York the next morning.

"Sam, mind that you serve Mr. Clay well or I'll warm your hide with my cane when I return!" said Mr. Leeds.

Then he took Sam's hand and shook it roughly. To Sam's amazement, the printer left a Spanish-milled dollar in his palm when he withdrew his hand.

"Don't get into any trouble with the British," Mr. Leeds told him. "They will be in command here for awhile. And remember! Mr. Clay will be held responsible for all you do."

"I'll be careful, sir," Sam promised. "Good luck to you and Mrs. Leeds on your journey."

As he watched them drive away, he was surprised to find himself feeling so forlorn and downhearted. But then the loft chamber had been his home for quite awhile now, and he had become accustomed to Mr. Leeds' crusty manner. Now he felt like a stray cat, left behind by one family and taken in by the kind people across the street. He sighed, then picked up the bundle that held his scanty possessions, and taking George under his arm, crossed the lane to the Clay house.

Mrs. Clay showed Sam the tiny room off the kitchen where he was to sleep. Sam arranged his things and then went over to the bookshop to ask Mr. Clay what his duties would be.

Mr. Clay was talking to Mr. Milton, who had come to say good-bye before following the other members of the Congress to York. His coach-and-four stood waiting in the street.

"You'll hear from me as soon as something can be arranged," Mr. Milton was saying, as Sam stepped into the shop.

How could they hear, Sam wondered, with the British holding Philadelphia?

The two men shook hands. Their solemn farewell was the old watchword of the Sons of Liberty, "God save our country!"

"It's a terrible thing to have Congress fleeing from Philadelphia again," Sam muttered, as Mr. Milton's coach rolled away.

Mr. Clay sighed deeply. Then he said, "Yes, and I fear that Lord Cornwallis and his troops will be here before sunset. Please ask Ellen and her mother to step over here. I want to have a serious talk with all of you."

Mr. Clay led Ellen, her mother, and Sam to his little office at the rear of the bookshop.

"The entire British Army will be quartered in or near Philadelphia," he told them gravely. "Some of the King's men will be coming to trade at the bookshop. I want all of you to treat them with courtesy."

Ellen turned pale. "But we just can't sell things to the enemy!" she burst out.

"The bookstore is our living," her uncle answered firmly. "I must keep it open, and if the British soldiers wish to trade here, we must serve them." His stern face turned from Ellen to Sam and back again to Ellen. "You will displease me very much if you do anything to anger our customers. We are all good Patriots here, but henceforth we will keep our political feelings to ourselves. Do you understand me, Ellen? Do you, Sam?"

"Yes, sir," Sam replied in a low voice. He felt as if the sky was crashing about them. How could a fine man like Mr. Clay play the part of a hypocrite — or worse?

Ellen had burst into tears. "I won't pretend that I'm a Tory!" she cried wildly.

Her uncle sighed and gave her shoulder a gentle pat. "I'm not asking you to be a Tory. Just try to keep your feelings to yourself." He turned to Sam. "I'll leave you in charge of the shop while I go out and see what news there is of the enemy."

After Mr. Clay had gone, Ellen and her mother lingered in the shop to discuss his strange new attitude toward the British.

"Let's try to do as he wishes without questioning his reasons," Mrs. Clay advised. "We must remember that he is keeping the shop open in order to earn a living for us."

The bell over the door tinkled to announce the entrance of a customer. When Sam hurried out of the office, he found a burly teamster standing in the shop.

"Is that Leeds' printshop across the way?" the man asked.

Through the open door of the bookshop, Sam could see a cart and a team of tired-looking horses standing before the closed and shuttered printshop.

"I've got a chap in my cart who says that he's a nephew of Mrs. Leeds," the teamster continued. "A mere lad he is, wounded at the Brandywine. I picked him up over Chester way, when a wagon loaded with our wounded broke down on the road. He begged me to bring him to the printshop. But the shop seems to be deserted, the house too, and I've got to leave the boy somewhere and get out of town quick!"

Sam rushed out of the door and across the lane. The wounded soldier couldn't be anyone but Joab Miller!

"He might be dead by this time," the teamster said cheerfully, as he strode after Sam. "He took an awful jolting."

The straw in the wagon was stained with blood, and so were the dirty rags wrapped around Joab's right arm. For the wounded soldier was indeed Joab. He lay so still and white that a stab of fear pierced Sam.

"He's fainted from pain," the teamster said.

"His aunt left town this morning," Sam said slowly.

"Well, you'll have to find someone to look after him, and be quick about it," the teamster insisted.

Mrs. Clay had followed them across the lane. Sam turned to her hopelessly. "It's Joab

Miller. Where can I hide him before the British come?"

"Why, in our house, of course." She shook her head sadly over Joab's condition.

"But Mr. Clay," Sam reminded her. "How's he going to feel about having a wounded Continental in his house, now that he's so anxious to stay in with the Redcoats?"

"If you abandon this boy to the enemy, they'll clap him into one of their filthy prisons to die of fever or hunger," the teamster said hotly. "And he'll die if he goes any further in this cart. He's lost a lot of blood."

"Please bring him into our house," said Mrs. Clay. "We'll put him in your room, Sam."

The teamster lifted Joab easily in his brawny arms and strode after Mrs. Clay, who led him around by the kitchen door and into Sam's little room. "There's a trundle bed upstairs that we will bring down for you, Sam," she said.

Joab groaned and opened his eyes. A faint grin flickered across his face when he saw Sam standing beside the bed looking down at him. "T-they got me again, Colonel Woodbury," he whispered. Then he recognized the teamster. "Thanks — mister — "

"These folks will take care of you," the man said gruffly. "I've got to hustle now — "

Mrs. Clay sent Sam and Ellen back to the bookshop while she cared for Joab's wound. She warned them not to breathe a word to Mr. Clay of Joab's presence in the house.

"Then, if we are caught caring for a Continental soldier, he can honestly say that we deceived him. But we won't get caught!" she added, seeing Sam's worried look. "We'll keep Joab hidden until he is well again, and then we'll find a way to get him back to our own army. Seth never comes into the kitchen, except for his meals, so if Joab takes care not to make a sound, no one will guess that he is here."

Sam felt guilty about deceiving Mr. Clay, but Joab had to be protected. That night, as the bookseller ate supper in the cozy kitchen of his home, he did not dream that a Continental soldier was lying in the next room.

But that was not the only excitement in Sassafras Lane that night. Someone broke into the Leeds' house and set it afire. No one knew whether the blaze was caused by one of Mr. Leeds' bitter enemies among the Tories, or whether it had been started accidentally by a tramp seeking shelter in the house. The Watch saw the blaze and roused the neighborhood, and the men and boys formed a bucket-line to several pumps. To Sam's surprise, old Mr.

Stone came and stood beside him and Mr. Clay in the bucket-line. He was glad to know that if Tories had set the fire, Mr. Stone had no part in the deed, because after all, he and Mr. Leeds had been friends before the war.

The bucket brigade saved the printshop, but by morning the little house stood a blackened shell in the midst of its trampled garden. Perhaps Mrs. Leeds would rather have had it that way, Sam thought sadly, than to know, as probably would have happened, that British soldiers were quartered inside her home.

George to the Rescue

WHEN the British Army marched into Philadelphia, the Patriots stayed off the streets,
but the happy Tories lined up to cheer the
soldiers and shout "God save the King!"

Bands filled the air with the clash of cym-
bals and the sounds of drums, fifes, and
trumpets. Bayonets sparkled, every musket
slanted at the same angle, every gaitered leg
flashed at exactly the same moment as the
King's grenadiers tramped along the streets.
Officers with gold lace on their hats and gold
braid thick upon their scarlet or green coats
bestrode prancing battle chargers.

The splendor of this army was in startling
contrast to the gaunt and ragged Continentals
who had paraded through Philadelphia only
a few days before.

General Howe established the main body
of his troops at Germantown, five miles out of
the city. He knew the Continentals were eager

to fight him again but he hoped to avoid another battle. The British losses had been so great at Brandywine that General Howe could not afford another such victory.

Then on an October day that brought bad luck to the Americans, General Washington made a spirited attack on the British at Germantown. The countryside was hidden under a thick curtain of fog. The Americans were driving the British back when two American regiments fired upon each other and once again, General Howe was able to snatch victory from defeat. But so battered and shaken was the British Army that Howe made haste to draw back inside the fortifications he had thrown up around Philadelphia.

The Continentals withdrew in good order. They knew it had been bad luck that had cost them the battle.

After Germantown, both armies were too exhausted to fight again. General Howe stayed at his fine headquarters in Philadelphia. General Washington and his men built a winter camp of log huts up the Schuylkill River at Valley Forge. There they could keep close tabs on the enemy in Philadelphia.

The Patriots of Philadelphia wondered uneasily what their fate would be with the British in possession of the town, but they soon discovered that General Howe was not a vindicative foe. The city was placed under military law, but Patriots who caused no trouble suffered no reprisal from the British.

One ill, however, the Patriots could not escape. The public buildings did not offer enough room to house all the British troops, and most of the officers had to be quartered with the people. It was only because their house was so small that the Clays escaped this, at least for a time.

As he had planned, Mr. Clay kept the bookshop open, and soon many British officers began to use it as a social club. To Sam's disgust, Mr. Clay did everything he could to make the officers comfortable. There was always a bright wood fire burning in the fireplace with a half-circle of chairs drawn up before it. The officers kept their long-stemmed clay pipes in a rack on the wall, and Mr. Clay had tobacco to sell them at a high price. While they sat smoking in the warmth of the fire, they talked freely of military affairs.

Mr. Clay never discussed the war and seemed to live only for his bookshop. Sometimes, however, it was necessary for Sam or Ellen to wait on customers. Out of gratitude toward Mr. Clay, Sam tried to do this with good grace, but Ellen could not conceal her true feelings. Still, this seemed to do no harm; when the good-natured officers discovered that Ellen admired General Washington, they teased her gently and called her a little rebel spitfire. Sam they barely noticed, which was fine with him.

By November, Joab Miller was recovered from his wound, and Sam, Ellen, and Mrs. Clay were perplexed by what to do about him. He could not remain much longer cooped up in the little room off the kitchen. It was a wonder that Mr. Clay had not already discovered him. After puzzling over ways of smuggling Joab out of Philadelphia, Sam decided to ask Tim Monroe for help.

The following morning he walked over to the Monroe house. Tim was in the stable rubbing down a white horse.

"Gaze upon the new horseboy and stableman to the officers of King George III, may he topple off his throne and black his royal eye!" Tim said with a crooked smile.

"Whose horse is that?" Sam glanced from the white charger to the other horses that were hanging their heads over the edge of the stalls. "Where's Chief? Where did you get these other horses?"

Tim led the white horse to its stall, then

stepped to the stable door to make sure that no one was listening to them. Satisfied, he invited Sam to sit down on an upended keg and pushed another close for himself.

"Chief is safe across the Schuylkill in the barn of a Patriot farmer. I got him out of town before the British arrived. It was the wisest act of my young life, because they've seized every decent nag they could lay hands on to mount their cussed dragoons. Oh, they pay for 'em in good British gold, but no amount of gold could pay me for the loss of Chief."

He waved his hand toward the stalls. "Those are the mounts of Colonel Dinwiddie and the other officers who are quartered at our house. You got any of them yet?"

Sam shook his head. "The Clay house is too small."

"They've taken our whole house — pushed the family into a couple of rooms. My mother has to cook for them and I've been appointed stableboy. They pay me, but I'm getting sick of it." He leaned closer and lowered his voice still more. "I'm going to make a break for freedom! I'll reach the American lines somehow and then go to York and work for the Congress again."

"I came over here to ask if you know any

way of getting out of town without a pass," Sam muttered.

"Do you want to go too?"

Sam sighed. "I've got to stay here. But you remember Joab Miller — " He poured out the story.

Tim was astounded. "All these weeks you've kept a Continental soldier hidden right under the noses of the British!"

"And under Mr. Clay's nose as well. But now we've got to get Joab out of there. Will you help us, Tim?"

"Of course," was Tim's prompt reply. "Joab can go with me."

He outlined his plan for escaping from the city. He had a cousin who lived on a small farm bordering the Schuylkill. Tim suspected him of being a Tory because he sold his produce regularly and willingly to the British.

"But the fact that they don't suspect him is all the better for us. I keep a canoe at his place for summer fishing on the river, and I haven't put it up yet this fall." Tim grinned widely. "Cousin John won't think it strange if I and a friend go out for one last fishing trip before I put the canoe in his barn. All Joab and I will have to do is land on the other bank, hide in the woods until dark, and then go to my friend's farm for Chief. Once we're up on

Chief, I'll wager that the British will never catch us."

"What about a pass to get you through the British lines and out to your cousin's farm?" Sam asked.

"That's easy. I'll just ask Colonel Dinwiddie for one and promise to bring him back some fish, if we catch any. He's fond of good eating."

"Tim, I believe you've hit it!" Sam said admiringly.

Tim nodded, pleased with himself. "I've told my mother and father and they agree that I should go. They'll be proud to have me riding for the Congress again."

Suddenly Sam looked troubled. "The British may take it out on your family when they find that you've skipped."

Tim shook his head. "Colonel Dinwiddie is a decent chap, even if he does wear a red coat, and my parents can't help it if I run away. To tell the truth, I think they'll breathe easier when I've left town. They're always worried that I'll get into trouble with our boarders. And believe me, Sam, it's plenty hard to keep my mouth shut when I hear some of the things the British say about General Washington and our army."

"I know what you mean," Sam said solemnly. "Plenty of times I've almost bitten my tongue off at the bookshop."

When Sam started home, plans had been made for the boys to make their getaway within a week. Saturday afternoon Tim came to the bookshop on the pretext of buying some sealing wax.

"Everything's arranged," he whispered to Sam. "Be sure Joab is ready about nine o'clock Tuesday morning. I'll stop by for him, because he doesn't know his way about town."

"Thanks, Tim. You're a good friend," Sam whispered back.

Monday morning Ellen was in the kitchen washing the breakfast dishes. Her mother was sewing on a hunting shirt she was making for Joab from a length of brown-dyed homespun. On the back of a chair was an old woolen cloak of Mr. Clay's which had been carefully mended.

"They say that our soldiers are half naked," Mrs. Clay said with a sigh. "You'll need all the clothing you can take with you, Joab. I've found you an extra pair of breeches, and you can conceal half-a-dozen pairs of woolen hose about your person."

Joab laughed light-heartedly. It seemed too good to be true that he was really going to get away. Grateful as he was to Sam and the

Clays, he could hardly wait to leave the stuffy little room behind and draw a breath of fresh air once more. And then there was always the fear of being discovered and dragged off to one of the fever-ridden, filthy British prisons, where many prisoners died of starvation and exposure.

Joab was sitting on the edge of his bed with the door open into the kitchen. Should Mr. Clay suddenly come into the kitchen, the bedroom door, hidden by the jog of the chimney, could be softly closed. Between his knees Joab held the iron shoe-last which Mr. Clay used to repair the family's everyday shoes. Beside him was a hammer and a handful of wooden pegs. He was carefully pegging a new leather sole on the pair of shoes that Tim had left for him on Saturday. The shoes that he had worn at Brandywine were so tattered that Mrs. Clay had thrown them out.

Ellen had just slid a pan of gingerbread into the fireside oven when the brass knocker clanged on the front door. She hurried along the hall that divided the house from the bookshop and opened the door. To her surprise a British officer was standing on the doorstep. Sudden fear made her heart beat faster. Officers were common enough at the bookshop, but why had this one come to the house? Had Joab's presence been discovered?

The officer smiled politely. "Is Mrs. Clay at home?"

"Come in, sir," Ellen replied stiffly. "I'll call her."

Spurs ajingle, he followed her into the parlor. Sam was there, mending the fire. At the sight of a British officer he almost dropped the log he was holding. Ellen's eyes flashed him a worried question. Then she asked the visitor to be seated and went to call her mother.

The officer seated himself in a comfortable chair near the fire. He smiled as his eyes fell on George, who was stretched out on the hearthrug.

"Quite a cat." he said. "What's the creature's name?"

"His name is George," Sam said shortly.

"George! 'Pon my word, 'tis a fitting name for a battered old tomcat with one ear chewed almost off." The officer laughed heartily. "Could it be you named him for Mr. Washington?"

Sam's mouth tightened. "Yes," he said firmly. "George is named after *General* Washington, and he's a gallant warrior, like the

94

General himself." He glared defiantly at the unwelcome visitor.

"Stab me! We have rebel sympathies, do we?"

"I'm an American, sir." For the life of him Sam could not have denied his patriotism, but he was glad that Mr. Clay was not there to hear him.

"I trust that your rash sentiments are not shared by your elders," snapped the officer.

"You'll have to ask them," Sam replied sullenly. "I'm only a bound boy."

Mrs. Clay's flurried entrance put an end to the conversation. The officer stood up and bowed. "I'm Major Darcy, at your service, ma'am."

She swept him a curtsey and waved him back to his chair. She sat down on the sofa, obviously worried as to what this was all about. Ellen stood beside her, and Sam lingered by the fireplace. George watched them all lazily.

"You wanted to see me?" Mrs. Clay prompted.

The major nodded. "Until now, I have lived at the barracks with my men, but now that we have captured the Delaware forts, and ships can come up the river, my wife is coming from New York to join me. Her ship docks tomorrow morning and I must have comfortable quarters for her. Your house was suggested to me by your neighbor, Mr. Stone, whom I met at a reception at General Howe's quarters."

Sam muttered angrily under his breath. Ellen looked crushed.

Mrs. Clay's fingers were nervously pleating the ruffle on her apron. "I'm afraid that we have no room for you, Major," she told him faintly.

"We will require only one bedroom and the parlor," was his firm reply. "You may serve our meals in here."

She stood up, her cheeks flushed with anger. "Indeed, sir, this house is barely large enough to accommodate our family."

"You may expect us in the morning," the major said, as if he had not heard her. He stood up. "Perhaps Mrs. Darcy will engage you as her personal maid," he said, smiling kindly at Ellen.

She stared at him, speechless.

"As for you, my lad," the officer continued, turning to Sam. "You will have the opportunity of seeing a real cat. Mrs. Darcy will be bringing our angora, Lorenzo the Magnificent."

"George doesn't like strange cats," Sam warned.

"Tut tut. Then poor old George will have to go. Until tomorrow, ma'am," he said to Mrs. Clay.

He marched out of the house.

"The silly popinjay!" Sam growled, scowling after him through the window. "I hope George eats his cat."

"Oh, Mother, what can we do?" Ellen cried.

"I'm afraid there is nothing we *can* do. We've been lucky until now."

"It's a good thing that Joab is leaving early tomorrow," said Sam. "It's going to be awful having that fellow ordering us about — and his wife — and cat — " He clenched his fists helplessly.

"I must go and talk this over with Seth." Mrs. Clay hurried from the room looking very much upset.

"Aren't you honored, Ellen," Sam said bitterly. "Her ladyship may allow you to serve her." He held out the side of his breeches and made an exaggerated curtsey. "Good morning, milady," he simpered. "Wouldst have me annoint the exalted whiskers of Lorenzo the Magnificent with a dash of rosewater?"

"I'll Lorenzo the Magnificent you!" Ellen shrieked. She darted at him and tugged at his hair. When he broke away with a howl of pain, she chased him around the room and along the hall to the kitchen.

Joab had his head thrust out of the bedroom door, dying to know what had happened in the parlor.

"Come out here and we'll tell you," Ellen said. "You can scoot into your room if we hear Uncle coming."

Joab sat down on the fireside settle, where the high back would hide him from anyone entering the room from the hall. He shook his head when they told him about Major Darcy. "It's high time that I left here. I could get you folks into a peck of trouble."

Just then Mrs. Clay swept into the room. "Seth is furious because the Darcys are coming here," she exclaimed. "I thought, in view of his friendliness with the officers who come to the shop, that he would be pleased."

Ellen looked surprised also, but a secret, satisfied smile crossed Sam's face.

A sharp knock sounded on the outside door. Not aware that Joab was in the kitchen, Mrs. Clay opened the door before he could escape into the bedroom. The caller was Mr. Stone, looking sour and angry and clutching his gold-headed cane. He stepped into the room and replied to Mrs. Clay's polite greeting with a grunt.

"Where's that boy? Where's that young thief?" he shouted. Sam was standing, much alarmed, between Joab and the door. Mr. Stone advanced upon him brandishing his cane. "I've a mind to break this over your back!"

"I wouldn't try it. And don't call me a thief!" Sam said angrily.

"You've been stealing my apples!"

"I haven't been near your apple shed."

"Then who was it that purloined a bushel of my best golden sweetings last night? Apples, mind you, that had been chosen especially for General Howe's own table."

"Perhaps General Howe came around in the night and fetched 'em home himself," Sam said with a grin.

Secretly, he had a suspicion that Carter Greene, the leader of the neighborhood boys, might have something to do with the disappearance of the apples. Sam didn't approve of such doings, even if Mr. Stone *was* a sour old Tory, but Carter's secret was safe with him.

"None of your sauce, boy!" Mr. Stone stormed. Suddenly his eyes lighted on Joab. Joab crossed his legs and tried to look unconcerned under the searching glance.

"Who are you?" Mr. Stone demanded. "I never saw you before."

His rudeness stirred Mrs. Clay's slow anger. "Are we obliged to inform you when we have a guest?" she asked sharply. "As for your apples, go and look elsewhere for the thief. Good day, sir."

But now Mr. Stone's suspicion had shifted to Joab. "I believe that the thief is no farther away than there, on your settle!" he shouted. "That fellow is a stranger, and I don't like his face."

"I don't like yours either," replied Joab, goaded beyond endurance.

"Mr. Stone, leave my house!" cried Mrs. Clay. She pointed to the door which was still standing open.

"Oh, I'll go. But you've not heard the last of this. A fine lot of gratitude you show me for recommending your house to a respectable officer of His Majesty's Army!"

"Thank you for nothing!" Sam flung after the old man, as he went stamping and muttering down the lane.

"Whew!" Joab brushed his sleeve across his damp forehead as Sam shut the door. "I was *scared*!"

"You shouldn't have been out of your room," Mrs. Clay scolded. Joab nodded guiltily.

"Don't worry," said Sam. "Mr. Stone may not like your face, but he doesn't suspect that you are a Continental soldier. And by this time tomorrow you'll be across the Schuylkill, on your way back to the army."

Mr. Clay came downstairs the next morning while Mrs. Clay was mixing the batter for breakfast waffles and Ellen was brewing a pot of blackberry and herb tea. The bookseller seemed to begrudge every daylight hour that he spent away from his shop. He would hurry over there every morning, as soon as he had finished his breakfast, and not return until dinnertime, when Sam took over tending the shop. This morning the three conspirators could hardly wait until he took himself off.

"Oh dear," Ellen sighed, as she ate a baked apple. "I can't bear to think of those Darcys living in our house."

"I hate to think of what George will do to that British cat, Alonzo, or whatever his silly name is," Sam muttered as he set George's breakfast bowl down on the hearthstone.

Mr. Clay got up from the table as if he could no longer relish his food.

"He's been moody and irritable ever since he heard that the Darcys are coming here," said Mrs. Clay, as the bookseller walked out of the room.

"I don't believe that Mr. Clay likes the

British as much as you think he does," Sam said with his secret smile.

Ellen peeped into the hall to make sure that her uncle really had gone to the shop. "It's safe for you to come out, Joab," she called softly, as she shut the door. She went to the fireplace and poured waffle batter on the hot iron.

While Joab ate his breakfast, Mrs. Clay stuffed the pockets of his jacket with woolen stockings and mittens.

"Did you put on those extra shirts, Joab?" she asked.

"Look at me!" he said with a chuckle. "What with all the layers of clothes, I'm round as a pumpkin."

Ellen was packing lunch in a bag. Sam went to the window and looked out anxiously, wishing that Tim would come. It had rained during the night and then turned very cold. The stone doorstep glistened with a coating of ice. It was getting too cold for fishing from a canoe, but Sam hoped that Colonel Dinwiddie wouldn't think of that.

Joab finished his breakfast and sat down on the settle, ready to grab his things and bolt out of the house the instant that Tim appeared. George curled up beside him for an after-breakfast snooze. "I'll miss you, George," Joab said. George began to purr and snuggled closer.

Suddenly everyone in the room seemed to freeze. Coach wheels were rolling over the frosty cobblestones of Sassafras Lane, a sound not often heard on that street. Sam uttered a groan of dismay that made Ellen run to join him at the window. "Oh!" she gasped. "Oh goodness! What shall we do?"

"What's the matter?" cried her mother.

"The Darcys!" Ellen hissed.

The coach had stopped before the front door of the house and a British soldier had jumped down from the box and opened the door. Out stepped Major Darcy. He helped a lady in a scarlet fur-lined cloak to alight, then he carefully lifted out a large wicker basket. With the lady on one arm and the basket on the other, he stepped over to the house door. The lady paused at the step with a scornful glance at the little red-brick house.

"Is this the best you could do for lodgings, Major?" she said reproachfully. "Surely this is not the fashionable part of town!"

"I did not have much time to look around, my dear. You will be comfortable here until I can find something more to your taste." He banged the door knocker.

Ellen turned wildly away from the window. "Quick, Joab, into the bedroom!" she yelped.

Mrs. Clay settled her cap firmly on her head.

"We must all stay calm," she declared, although she herself was shaking. "Ellen, answer the door and show the Darcys right upstairs! The rest of us will stay here until Tim arrives."

Ellen ran along the hall and jerked the door open. Mrs. Darcy gave her a stately nod as she swept into the hall. The major followed with a pleasant "good morning." From the wicker basket floated a plaintive *"Meow."* The major's orderly marched in the rear with Mrs. Darcy's brassbound trunk balanced on one shoulder.

"Take the trunk upstairs!" ordered the major. He set the basket on the hall table and fumbled with the catch. When the orderly came downstairs, he ordered him to go to the barracks and fetch his luggage.

Loud yowls were coming from the basket.

"Do hurry, Major," cried Mrs. Darcy. "Poor Lorenzo is so cramped in that wretched basket. And he was seasick all the way from New York."

"Tch, tch," sympathized her husband. At last the latch came loose. The major reached into the basket and lifted out a large black cat with a pink bow around its neck.

Mrs. Darcy took the cat in her arms. "My

precious Lorenzo," she cooed. "Are you hungry?"

"*Meow-ow!*" wailed Lorenzo.

"He must have some warm cream at once, Major."

"I'll take him to the kitchen and feed him with my own hands," the major promised.

To Ellen's horror, he took the cat and started for the kitchen door with Mrs. Darcy mincing behind him.

"Lorenzo isn't used to eating in a kitchen," the lady protested. The major paid her no heed. He pushed the kitchen door open. Peering past him, Ellen saw with relief that Sam and her mother were alone in the room. They stared at the Darcys and their cat in amazement.

"My good woman," the major said to Mrs. Clay. "Kindly warm some cream for Mrs. Darcy's cat."

Lorenzo began to struggle. He had never been in a kitchen before but he liked the warmth of it and the smell of good food. He jumped to the floor and stood waving his plumy tail and meowing for his cream.

George had been fast asleep on the settle but the sound of a strange cat's voice aroused him from his slumber. He sat up. His ears flattened and his tail twitched ominously. Had some rash animal actually dared to invade his premises? His topaz eyes shot out sparks of fire as they focused on Lorenzo. What kind of cat was this, all tied up with pink ribbon? With a yowl of disgust he jumped off the settle and flung himself fiercely on the stranger.

Lorenzo was taken aback by the whirlwind attack but he put up a feeble show of resistance. The two cats spun around the kitchen, clawing, spitting, and shrieking their hatred of each other.

"Oh, Major, *do* something!" screamed Mrs. Darcy.

She collapsed on the settle with her hands over her face. Mrs. Clay sent Ellen running for the smelling salts.

"Call off your cat, boy!" the major roared at Sam. The two of them were dancing about, trying to catch hold of their fighting pets.

"George, stop that!" Sam shouted, quite without result. He grabbed at the black and golden pinwheel of raking claws and punishing teeth and got his hands well clawed.

Ellen came hurrying back with the smelling salts. As she handed the bottle to her mother, she glanced out of the window. Tim Monroe was coming along the lane! Ellen snatched Joab's bundle of lunch off the table and jerked open the bedroom door. "Quick! Here's Tim!" she hissed.

Joab had his hat and coat on. He grabbed the bundle as he shot past Ellen, muttering words of gratitude and farewell. Before Tim had a chance to knock at the door, it opened and Joab shot out. "Double quick!" he cried. "We've been boarded by the enemy."

Skidding on the icy step, Tim whipped about-face. The two boys started to hurry along the lane and almost collided with Mr. Stone, who was coming to tell Mrs. Clay that a gang of boys had thrown some dead rats over his fence the night before. He was sure that Sam was the ringleader. But the sight of Tim and Joab drove the rats out of his mind. He had been suspicious of the strange boy the day before, but now, seeing him with Tim Monroe, a messenger for the traitorous Continental Congress, he decided that Joab was a spy.

"Halt!" he shouted. He clutched at Joab as the boy sprinted past him. "In the name of the King!"

Joab pulled free and he and Tim legged it desperately along the lane and disappeared around the corner.

"Help!" yelled Mr. Stone. "A spy! A rebel spy!"

He was answered from the house, but not in the way that he expected. Joab had left the door open. Now Lorenzo the Magnificent shot through it in an attempt to escape from the terrible yellow beast who had attacked him. After Lorenzo rushed his master.

"Stop him!" bellowed the major as Lorenzo streaked between Mr. Stone's legs, almost upsetting him.

The amazed and flustered old gentleman grabbed wildly at Lorenzo's tail. Lorenzo shrieked in agony but continued his flight, with George in hot pursuit. The major skidded across the icy doorstep, and feeling himself falling, clutched at Mr. Stone and pulled him down also.

"Let go!" clamored Mr. Stone. " 'Tis yon spy fellow making off up the lane you want to catch — not me!"

Major Darcy struggled to his feet with a dazed look on his face. Sam ran out and helped Mr. Stone up. In the kitchen, Mrs. Darcy went into screaming hysterics. Ellen pushed the smelling salts under her nose again.

"Look at my hat!" stormed Mr. Stone, picking his fine beaver off the doorstep. "Flat as a penny! 'Pon my word, Darcy, you must have sat on it."

"My cat!" the major cried, glancing frantically around.

"No, no — my hat!" shouted Mr. Stone. "You've ruined it! And the spy — we're forgetting him. He ran down the lane. *No, no!* In the other direction!" he shrieked, as Major Darcy took off across the lane and into the garden of the Leeds' house. *"You're letting the spy escape, Major!"* The old man was fairly hopping up and down in rage.

"Joab isn't a spy," Sam assured him mildly. "And anyhow, your friend Major Darcy isn't interested in anything just now except Lorenzo the Magnificent."

Mr. Stone's jaw dropped. "Lorenzo the Magni — Are ye daft, boy?"

Sam grinned. "Lorenzo is Mrs. Darcy's cat and our George has him treed in the maple in Mr. Leeds' yard."

Mr. Stone scowled across the lane. Sure enough, there was Major Darcy standing beneath the maple, begging his cat to come down. The boy was right. Incredible as it seemed, the major was more interested in a wretched cat than in doing his duty as a British officer.

"Chasing a cat while rebel spies swarm under his nose," Mr. Stone muttered. "General Howe will hear of this, I assure you!"

Clapping his crushed hat on, he limped toward his own house and was confronted by George, who was sitting on the fence, happily removing tufts of black fur from his claws. A thread of pink ribbon dangled from his whiskers. "Scat, you cat!" roared Mr. Stone.

"George, come here!" Ellen ran over and took the now purring cat in her arms. "You'd better get out of sight." She made for the bookshop door. As she passed Sam they exchanged happy glances. Tim Monroe knew every alley and shortcut in town, and they could be sure that the boys were safely on their way to the river.

With his hands in the pockets of his breeches and his lips pursed in a soundless whistle, Sam strolled across the lane to the Leeds' yard. Lorenzo was clinging to a high branch of the big maple, wailing mournfully. The major greeted Sam with a frown.

"Get up in this tree and bring my cat down!" he commanded. "Mind you handle him gently! I'll attend to that animal of yours later."

Sam looked him squarely in the eyes. "If you want me to get your cat, you'll have to promise not to harm George. I warned you that George wouldn't want a strange cat around, so it's your own fault that he attacked Lorenzo."

"I refuse to bargain with you!" said the angry officer. "That cat of yours is a dangerous beast. He should be destroyed."

Sam turned on his heel. "I guess you'll have to get a soldier from the barracks to bring Lorenzo down," he said over his shoulder.

This gave the major pause. He knew that if this ridiculous story ever got about, his fellow officers would never stop laughing at him. And also, if he didn't get Lorenzo down quickly, there would be a terrible scene with Mrs. Darcy.

"Wait, boy," he said in a milder tone. "Climb up and get Lorenzo. I'll not harm your cat. Once Lorenzo is safe, I want to forget this whole affair."

Sam turned back. "On your honor as an officer and a gentleman?" he asked.

"On my honor," Major Darcy assured him solemnly.

Sam jumped to catch a low branch and climbed up the tree. Reaching Lorenzo's lofty perch, he spoke to the cat in a gentle voice and Lorenzo seemed to understand that here was a person who liked cats. He allowed Sam to edge closer. Sam jerked off his shirt, wrapped the trembling cat in it, and slid back down the trunk. With a groan of relief the major snatched Lorenzo from him.

"You've given your word about George," Sam reminded him.

Major Darcy nodded grimly. He marched back across the lane with Lorenzo cuddled in his arms and Sam walking jauntily at his heels. A window in the Stone house was flung open and Mr. Stone thrust his head out and began to upbraid the major for having allowed a spy to escape.

"And General Howe will hear of it if you do not pay for my hat!" he yelled.

The Clay door banged behind the major, Lorenzo, and Sam.

Mrs. Clay had succeeded in soothing Mrs. Darcy, but when the major's wife saw her cat, she burst into tears. Lorenzo, alas, was no longer "The Magnificent." His ribbon was in tatters, there was a nick in one of his ears, and the spirit was utterly gone out of him. With a sob Mrs. Darcy gathered him in her arms. "Oh, Major," she moaned. "Take us away from this dreadful place."

"Immediately, my dear." The major was only too happy to leave a neighborhood that he was firmly convinced was inhabited by lunatics. "When the coach returns with my baggage, we'll drive to an inn and stay there until we can find a suitable dwelling." He turned to

Mrs. Clay. "What means all this clamor about spies, ma'am?"

She lifted her head proudly. " 'Tis true that Tim Monroe is an ardent Patriot, but that does not make him a spy."

"And what of the other boy?"

"A friend of Sam's who has been visiting us."

Mrs. Darcy came back from the hall, where she had fastened Lorenzo inside his basket. "Pray let us go," she said, "before that savage wildcat returns to attack Lorenzo again."

The major gave her his arm. He really had nothing of which to accuse the two boys, and he imagined that Mr. Stone's bitter feeling toward Patriots might have prompted him to use the term spy without just cause. Remembering how the man had insisted that he, Major Darcy, had ruined his hat, the major decided that not much reliance could be placed on his opinions.

"Let us go," he said to his wife.

When Mrs. Clay returned to the kitchen, after seeing the Darcys off, she found George in his place on the fireside settle with Sam and Ellen.

"Isn't he wonderful, Mother!" Ellen exclaimed. "He got rid of the Darcys for us.

Congress ought to give him a medal as a Patriot cat."

"What's been going on here?" Mr. Clay demanded suddenly from the doorway. "Why hasn't Sam come over to the shop this morning? And did my eyes deceive me, or was that Major Darcy and his wife driving away just now?"

"They've gone and they're not coming back," Ellen told him happily. "Mrs. Darcy won't let her precious cat stay under the same roof with George."

Mr. Clay's face brightened and he rubbed his hands together, as he did when he was pleased. There was no doubt that he was as happy as the rest of the family over the departure of the Darcys.

About a week after that exciting day in Sassafras Lane, Sam walked over to the Monroe house to see Tim's mother.

"Oh, it's you, Sam!" she said with a welcoming smile, when he stepped into the kitchen. Her face was flushed and her mobcap was slightly askew as she bustled about getting dinner for her unwelcome British guests. She moved close to Sam and put her hand on his shoulder.

"Word has come through, don't ask me how, that Tim and your friend got safely through

114

the enemy lines," she whispered. "Tim has gone to York, and the Miller boy has rejoined his regiment at Valley Forge."

Sam's relief showed in the wide smile he gave Mrs. Monroe.

All the way home, though, he kept wondering how the word from Tim had reached Tim's mother. It was said that General Washington had a carefully worked out intelligence system, but even so it seemed almost impossible that a message from the American camp could get through the tight British lines into occupied Philadelphia.

Mystery at the Bookshop

ONE morning in February, Sam was whistling "Yankee Doodle" as he stacked logs in the woodbox beside the fireplace in the bookshop. Outside, icicles framed the many-paned window, where George was sprawling contentedly.

"You'd better not let Uncle Seth hear you whistling that song!" Ellen snapped. She scowled as she wiped a dustcloth along a shelf of books. It still hurt and shamed her that her beloved uncle was no longer the Patriot that he once had been.

Sam's gray eyes narrowed. "I still can't believe that Mr. Clay is any more fond of the enemy than we are, Ellen."

He broke off as the bell above the door tinkled to announce the entrance of a customer. The young man who stepped in out of the cold was wearing heavy boots, a woolen smock, and a fur cap. He looked like most of the farmers who brought potatoes, turnips, and such to the city market, but Sam felt there was something vaguely different about him. The proud set of his broad shoulders seemed to smack more of the army than of following a plough.

The man asked for an almanac. Sam was getting one from the shelf when Mr. Clay stepped through the door that connected with the house.

"A good morning to you, sir," the farmer drawled.

As Sam turned away from the shelf with the almanac in his hand, he caught a look of understanding between this stranger and Mr. Clay.

"Here's the book you want," he said to the farmer. The man pulled off his mittens and thumbed through the pages. "I don't believe I want it after all," he muttered.

Then he handed the almanac, not to Sam, but to Mr. Clay, who opened a drawer under the counter and thrust the book inside. He had just closed the drawer when the bell tinkled again and Major Darcy stepped into the shop.

Since he and Mrs. Darcy had found comfortable quarters elsewhere, the major had forgiven Sam and the Clays the uproar over the two cats. Sam greeted him with a grin. "How is Lorenzo the Magnificent, sir?"

"Very well," replied the major with a frosty

twinkle in his eyes. "And I trust that your George is the same."

The farmer turned to take his leave. "And so I'll not be able to deliver your firewood until my next trip to town," he said to Mr. Clay, as if they had been discussing firewood instead of almanacs. "They took my entire load at the barracks."

Major Darcy gave the man a searching glance. "Are you the owner of the sledge standing before this shop?"

"Yes, sir. I've just delivered some wood to the barracks."

"Let me see your pass!"

Sam's heart began to beat faster. He knew that the British had to issue many passes to country people who brought food and firewood into Philadelphia, and that the British closely watched the movements of these people, because they suspected that some of them were spies for General Washington. Now Sam bit his lip in apprehension. What if the man was a Patriot spy? What if he had no pass?

Sam watched uneasily while the farmer fumbled through his pockets. Finally the man pulled out a much-folded bit of paper and handed it to Major Darcy. The major peered at it suspiciously.

"George Brooks may be passed through the lines to carry wood into Philadelphia," he read. "Hmmm." He examined the signature closely and then tossed the paper back to Brooks. "Everything seems to be in order. But be on your way, fellow! Country people are not permitted to loiter about town."

The farmer nodded and slouched to the door.

"Why," Sam thought in surprise, "he doesn't walk like a soldier after all!"

"Be sure to bring me some wood on your next trip to town," Mr. Clay called after the farmer.

Major Darcy stood at the window watching Brooks drive away in the sledge behind a plodding white horse.

"May I serve you, Major?" asked Mr. Clay.

The major nodded. "Give me a couple of the latest novels for Mrs. Darcy, and a ream of the best Dutch paper."

Mr. Clay picked two novels from a shelf, then stepped over to the cupboard where paper was kept. "Half a ream is all I can let you have," he said. "Paper is scarce, due to the war. We have to import all our writing paper from Europe, you know. The product of our American mills is still too coarse to be used for anything but newsprint."

"But it's getting better all the time," Sam put in. He flushed in confusion as Major Darcy turned to stare at him.

"Are you an authority on paper, boy?"

"I ought to be. I'm a printer's apprentice."
Sam felt like kicking himself as Mr. Clay
threw him a provoked look.

"Is this boy your nephew, Mr. Clay?" the
major asked.

"No. Sam is not related to us. He was apprenticed to Mr. Leeds, the master printer,
whose shop is across the lane."

The major knit his brows. "James Leeds,
who was one of those who printed the treasonable Declaration of Independence?"

Mr. Clay nodded curtly. "But we can't
blame the boy for his master's misdeeds," he
said, ignoring the outraged expression on
Sam's face. "When the King's army took Philadelphia, Leeds closed his shop and fled. Sam
is an orphan, so we invited him to live with
us. He's a great help to me in the shop."

"Well, Sam," Major Darcy said. "Now I
know from whence springs your admiration
for the traitor George Washington. You are
lucky to have exchanged a treasonable master
for one who is loyal to the King."

Sam almost choked on the fury he dared
not show. He saw Ellen glaring at the major,
her cheeks flaming, her hands clenched angrily
on her duster. Mr. Clay must have felt uneasy
about what they might say next for he spoke
to them sharply. "Ellen, see if your mother

needs you! Sam, fill the woodboxes in the house!"

Ellen tossed her head and flounced out of the shop. Sam followed, but he had only started to fill the kitchen woodbox when Mr. Clay opened the hall door and shouted, "Ellen! Sam! Come in here, please."

Major Darcy had left and the bookseller was alone. Mr. Clay led the way to his office. Sam noticed that there was an almanac on the desk. Could it be the one that George Brooks had fingered that morning?

Ellen's downcast face showed that she still resented the scene with Major Darcy in the bookshop. Her uncle smiled and put his arm around her.

"Sam and Ellen," he said in a low voice. "I am going to give you a chance to serve your country."

A tingle ran down Sam's spine. Ellen's lips parted.

"I have just received a message from my friend, Mr. Milton," Mr. Clay continued.

"But Mr. Milton is in York!" Ellen exclaimed.

"And now you are wondering how he managed to get word to me through the British lines."

Sam was staring at the almanac. He thought

121

of how George Brooks had thumbed through the book before he handed it to Mr. Clay, and how swiftly the bookseller had whisked it out of sight. He glanced up to find that the bookseller was watching him.

"I think that you are beginning to figure out one way that the Congress and General Washington send messages into Philadelphia," Mr. Clay said.

Sam nodded. "Something mysterious just had to be going on at the bookshop! I knew there had to be a good reason why you made the British so welcome here. And then, last week, I was in the shop when a farmer came in and asked for a book he didn't buy, and when George Brooks did the same thing — "

"You're a bright boy, Sam." Mr. Clay shook his head in a troubled way. "I pray no one else has been so observant."

"I don't think anyone else has noticed anything."

"Well, you at least have stumbled on our secret. George Brooks is not a farmer. He made me a secret sign by which I recognized him as one of General Washington's intelligence force — daring men who come into the city to gather information for the General and to bring his instructions to American secret agents here, of which I am one."

Ellen threw her arms around his neck and kissed him. "So *that's* why you are friendly with the British. They'd never dream of looking for spies in your shop!"

"I hope not," her uncle said seriously. "And also, our own people can come openly to a shop without arousing suspicion. But I had an uneasy moment this morning when Major Darcy happened in while Brooks was here. It was Brooks who brought the message from Mr. Milton and left it in the almanac, as you guessed, Sam. It concerns General Washington's desperate need for money with which to purchase food for the army. I'm going to give you the chance to help obtain those desperately needed food supplies, Sam."

While Sam stared at him eagerly, Mr. Clay got up and looked out into the shop to make sure that no one was there. Sam and Ellen crowded close to him when he returned to his chair.

"Last autumn, Mr. Milton, who is a very wealthy man, collected five thousand dollars in gold for the army," Mr. Clay told them. "But before he was able to get the gold to General Washington, Congress had to flee from the city. He dared not take the gold with him, for fear he might be captured, so before he left I helped him to hide it in his house. Now he wants me to get the gold and send it to General Washington by George Brooks, who will call for it here at the shop."

"But I've heard that there are British officers quartered in Mr. Milton's house!" Sam exclaimed.

"I know, Sam. That is why I cannot go after the gold myself, so I'm asking you to go for me. I'll get you into the house without causing any suspicion."

Sam felt a qualm of uneasiness. What would the British do to him, if they caught him poking around in their quarters looking for gold? Then he reminded himself sharply that the important thing was to get the gold to General Washington, and never mind what might happen to himself.

"Will you risk it, Sam?" Mr. Clay asked.

"I'll be proud to go, sir," Sam said quickly. "And if the gold is still in the house, I'll fetch it. But the British may have found it."

"I doubt that. We hid it well, but in a place where you can get at it easily, once you are living in the house."

"I'm to live there? How will you manage that?"

"Mr. Milton's servants are still there, looking after the property. The British officers kept them on, when they took the house over.

It would be natural for them to wish to hire some extra help," Mr. Clay explained. "I'll write Dan Andrews a note, asking him to hire you, and sign Mr. Milton's initials under my name, so that he'll know that the request really comes from him. Although he is trustworthy and a firm Patriot, Dan knows nothing about the hidden gold, and it will be best for him and Mrs. Andrews if we do not let them into the secret. Then if anything goes wrong, they cannot be blamed."

"What can I do to help?" Ellen asked, feeling rather out of things.

"With Sam away, you'll have more to do in the bookshop," her uncle said. "You must listen carefully to what the officers talk about, so that if they let drop any bit of information that might be of value to General Washington, you can repeat it to me. Also, if I have to get in touch with Sam, you are the only one I could trust to carry the message."

Sam shuffled his feet impatiently. "You haven't told me where the gold is hidden," he reminded Mr. Clay.

"It's in the library in two old law books. We cut out the insides of the books and hid half of the gold in each volume. With the covers glued down, they look like any other books. We hid them behind a collection of the

Sermons of Jonathan Edwards, on the top shelf in a corner of the library. You have only to seize a moment when no one is near and climb up and get them. But the books are heavy!" Mr. Clay warned. "Each one contains two thousand, five hundred dollars in gold and weighs nearly ten pounds. Hide them under your bed and then slip out and bring them here, one at a time."

Sam wondered if getting that gold out would be as easy as Mr. Clay made it sound.

"You won't have much time," Mr. Clay continued. "George Brooks will be coming for the gold within a fortnight."

The following morning, Sam walked over to the Milton house at the edge of town. He went up a brick walk between two rows of boxwood hedge and thumped the knocker on the kitchen door. The knock was answered by a middle-aged man in a neat black suit.

"Are you Mr. Andrews?" Sam asked. When the man nodded, he handed him Mr. Clay's note.

Mr. Andrews gave him a sharp glance and then invited him into the kitchen. Sam waited in silence while the man broke the wax seal on the folded paper. He read the note and then tossed it into the fireplace and watched until it had burned to ashes.

"Well, boy," he said to Sam. "You come well recommended, and I guess we can use another pair of hands in this house."

Sam swallowed hard. Now that he was actually in the house with the gold, the task ahead loomed difficult and dangerous. He made a silent promise to the men at Valley Forge that come what may, he would not let them down.

"Hang your cap and jacket behind the door," Mr. Andrews directed. "You come at a good time. The colonel's orderly, who used to help with the work, fell on the ice and broke his leg, and is now in the hospital. You can begin your duties by carrying hot water to the gentlemen upstairs. Serve Colonel Watts first. He's in the large chamber next to the library, at the front of the house."

While he was speaking bells had begun to jingle from the rooms of the British officers quartered in the house. Sam was soon on the run, carrying pitchers of hot water, polishing boots, brushing fine red uniform coats, and later, trotting back and forth between the kitchen and the stately dining room with pots of tea and plates of hot muffins and waffles. He didn't even have time to take a peep inside the library during those first hectic hours.

Hidden Gold!

THERE were four British officers staying in Mr. Milton's house. Lieutenant Carvel and Lieutenant Percy were jolly young men; they were prone to tip the new boy servant generously when he performed some service for them. Sam thought that he could have liked these two very well, if they had not been enemies of his country.

Captain Lynnwood was cross and overbearing and demanded more service than all the others put together. Sam feared his sharp, suspicious eyes.

Colonel Watts, the senior officer, was portly and grave but not unkind. Unfortunately, he was subject to severe attacks of the gout and he spent much of his time in an armchair in the library with his gouty foot propped up on a cushion. Late on his first morning in the house, Sam was sent up to the library with a tray for the colonel. While he was pouring coffee and passing the plate of buttered muffins, he let his eyes roam over the bookshelves. He soon located the set of Edwards' *Sermons* on the top shelf in a dim corner. They looked as if they had not been disturbed in years. There was a little stepladder in another corner. Sam itched to mount it and explore behind the sermons to see if the "gold books" were still safe.

As the days passed, he realized that he wasn't going to find it easy to get the library to himself. When Colonel Watts was out, Captain Lynnwood seemed to be forever prowling about in there, admiring the handsome books and pulling them out to examine them. Sam decided that he would have to get at the books late at night, when the officers were asleep in their rooms.

He himself had no room. He slept on the high-backed fireside settle in the kitchen, with a thick quilt folded under him and another quilt to cover him.

On Sam's third night in the Milton house both Colonel Watts and Captain Lynnwood went early to bed. Sam felt that his chance had come. Mr. and Mrs. Andrews had gone to their chamber on the third floor soon after supper was cleared away. Sam lighted two candles in brass holders and left them on the table in the hall for the younger officers, who often stayed out late. He laid some slow-burning logs on the kitchen fire, to hold it during the night, then he pulled off his shoes and huddled himself in his quilt to wait.

His head was nodding when he heard the two lieutenants come in and go upstairs. Soon the house was dark and still. Sam crouched on the settle, tense with excitement. He must give the officers time to fall asleep. The moments dragged on and the glow from the logs in the fireplace grew misty before his eyes. He yawned and his head fell forward on his chest, then suddenly he jerked upright, awakened by the musical chime of the tall Rittenhouse clock on the stairs.

The clock was striking four. Silvery moon-light was glimmering through the frost flowers on the windowpanes. The only sound, after the clock was still, was a mouse scurrying across the floor. Sam drew a deep breath and got to his feet. It was now or never!

Soft-footed in his thick woolen hose, he stole into the hall at the front of the house. Moonlight was spilling in through the window on the landing. Sam crept up the gleaming pathway. By going up the front stairs, he avoided passing the rooms occupied by the lieutenants at the back of the upstairs hall.

His heart was drumming loudly in his ears by the time he reached the upper hall. As he crept past Captain Lynnwood's room a board creaked sharply underfoot. Sam gasped and froze in his tracks, expecting the captain to rush out and challenge him. Nothing happened, so after a moment he moved cautiously on past Colonel Watts' room. Loud snores assured him that the colonel was fast asleep.

The library door stood open. Sam pussyfooted inside and shut the door. He leaned against it a moment, breathing deeply in his relief at having made it this far undetected.

Red velvet curtains, partly drawn, shut out all but a faint gleam of moonlight from the big, book-lined room. Sam waited until his eyes grew accustomed to the dimness, then he groped his way to the corner where the little ladder was kept. He located the ladder when he bumped his toe against it. He bit back a yelp of pain and stood on one foot and nursed his bruised toe between both hands. Then urged by the necessity for haste, he lugged the stepladder to the corner where the Edwards' books sat high on their shelf. He mounted cautiously and balanced on the top step while he reached out for one of the books of sermons.

"Stand! Ho there! Stand, I say!"

Sam was so startled by the shouts that he had to grab at a shelf to prevent himself from falling. Another bellow echoing through the dark house sent him backing hastily down the ladder. The voice was coming from the colonel's room. Had Colonel Watts become aware of his presence in the library? He tiptoed to the door, opened it a crack, and crouched in the shadows, trembling.

Captain Lynnwood and the two lieutenants had tumbled out of their beds. Barefooted, wearing nightshirts and tassled nightcaps, and carrying swords in their hands, they rushed to the aid of their colonel.

"What's amiss, sir?" Sam heard Captain Lynnwood demand.

Sam stepped cautiously into the hall and peered into the bedroom. The captain had struck a flint and lighted the candle on the bedside candlestand. Colonel Watts was sitting up in his curtained bed, his nightcap askew as he stared groggily at the three men standing at his bedside with drawn swords.

"Wha — what's all this about?" he sputtered.

"You shouted, sir," Lieutenant Carvel told him.

"I did?" The colonel pushed back his night-

132

cap. "I must have had a nightmare," he muttered.

In the hall, Sam went weak with relief. The shouts had nothing to do with him, after all.

"I thought that it must have been a rebel spy at the least," Captain Lynnwood rapped out, cross because his superior officer had disturbed his rest.

The colonel glared at him. "Go down to the kitchen and bid that boy stir me up a noggin of hot grog," he ordered.

Cold with terror lest he be caught out of bed, Sam skimmed along the hall, hugging the shadows. Before Captain Lynnwood had left the colonel's room, Sam had reached the top of the stairs. He vaulted astride the rail and whizzed down noiselessly, and by the time the captain had reached the kitchen, he was stretched out on the settle with the quilt over him. The captain shook his shoulder to wake him.

"Get up and carry a noggin of hot grog to the colonel!"

Sam's heart was heavy as he heated the drink. He dared not make another attempt to get at the gold that night, yet time was flying. If the gold wasn't at the bookshop when George Brooks came to fetch it, there might not be another chance to send it to General Washington.

The following afternoon Sam answered a rap on the front-door knocker. Ellen was standing on the doorstep, bright-eyed and pretty in a red, hooded cloak. She stared at him as if she had never seen him before.

"Is Lieutenant Carvel in?" she asked, nose in air.

"Pray step inside, miss." Sam winked solemnly and Ellen winked back. Her lips quirked and Sam realized that she was ready to burst into giggles. He shook his head sternly, then left her in the hall and stepped into the drawing room, where Lieutenant Carvel was playing cards with some friends. The lieutenant excused himself and followed Sam back to the hall. Ellen dropped a curtsey and held out a little book.

" 'Tis the copy of Mr. Goldsmith's *Vicar of Wakefield* that you ordered from my uncle, Mr. Clay," she explained.

"Ah, yes. Thank you, my pretty moppet." The young man took the book and turned to Sam. "Take the maid to the kitchen and ask Mrs. Andrews to give her some sweetmeats."

Sam led the way to the back of the hall. In the shadow under the stairs Ellen caught hold of his sleeve.

"Uncle Seth is getting anxious. Have you found you-know-what?"

He shook his head glumly. "I know where it is, but I haven't been able to get my hands on it."

"Well, you'd better hurry," Ellen warned.

Sam pushed her ahead of him through the kitchen door. Mrs. Andrews, a thin, tired-looking woman, was bending over the fireplace, stirring a great kettle of chicken stew.

"This is Ellen Clay," said Sam. "Lieutenant Carvel wants you to give her some sweetmeats."

Mrs. Andrews hung up her long-handled spoon. Her usually pleasant mouth was set in a tight line. "As if I don't have enough to do without handing out sweetmeats to every saucy minx who comes along!" she scolded.

It was plain that she was in a temper about something. Ellen backed toward the door. "Indeed I have no wish to trouble you, ma'am." Her cheeks were pink from embarrassment.

Mrs. Andrews' expression softened. " 'Tis not you who trouble me," she said. "Sit down, my dear. Sam, fetch a mug of milk for your friend, and one for yourself as well. You need it, goodness knows, the way you are expected to run your legs off waiting on our fine gentlemen. But just wait! 'Tis they who'll be running next spring, when General Washington sets out after them."

She cut two generous slices from a freshly baked nut cake, and while the young people were eating, she poured out her woes.

Captain Lynnwood had been recalled to England and the other three officers were planning to give him a farewell dinner party to which they were inviting some other British officers and also some of the rich Tories of Philadelphia. "They expect me to cook a fancy dinner for almost thirty people," Mrs. Andrews complained bitterly.

"Could I be of help to you?" Ellen asked impulsively. "I can make pastry, turn the meat upon the spit, and oh, do lots of things."

"Why bless your heart! I'll be glad to have your help," Mrs. Andrews replied.

The hall door opened and Mr. Andrews came stamping into the kitchen.

"Here's a fine to-do!" he stormed. "I heard Captain Lynnwood asking Colonel Watts for permission to take some of Mr. Milton's books back to England. At first the colonel refused, saying that he would not allow the King's officers to loot private homes, but when Captain Lynnwood reminded him that Mr. Milton is a member of the Continental Congress, the colonel changed his mind and declared that a traitor deserves to lose his property." The loyal servant clenched his hands helplessly. "Mr. Milton will be beside himself when he hears of the theft of his books!"

The news upset Sam even more than it had Mr. Andrews. What if the captain's fancy should light on the books of sermons and he removed them from the shelf, bringing to view the treasure books behind them? The very idea made him feel desperate.

"I'll try to get the gold tonight," he whispered to Ellen, when she was leaving.

But that night the colonel and Captain Lynnwood played chess in the library, and after the colonel had gone to bed, the captain stayed in his easy chair before the fire and read until the small hours of the morning. Sam crept up the stairs time after time only to see candlelight still glowing in the library. Waiting for the captain to go to bed, he fell asleep huddled on the bottom step. When he awoke, cramped and shivering with cold, the pale light of early morning was stealing in through the fanlight over the front door and Mr. and Mrs. Andrews were coming down the attic stairs to begin the day's work.

He had failed again.

Later that day, Captain Lynnwood started to choose the books he wanted and Sam was ordered up to the library to help him pack them. The captain strolled around the room, peering at the shelves of books through his quizzing glass. He pulled out the books he wanted and tossed them to Sam to be packed in a large barrel. Finally he reached the corner where Edwards' *Sermons* were ranged on the highest shelf. Sam watched him in almost unbearable suspense.

The captain examined a rare old volume of Shakespeare's sonnets, which had been brought to America by Mr. Milton's grandparents when they settled in the new little colony of Penn's Woods. "A choice find!" he exulted.

He handed the book to Sam to be packed, then to Sam's horror, he stepped back and stared up at the Edwards books. "What have we here?" he murmured. "Boy, bring the ladder and get me one of those books on the top shelf!"

Sam crossed the room on dragging feet.

"Step lively!" the captain commanded. "You move like a man of eighty."

Sam set the ladder in place and climbed slowly to the top step. He reached hopefully for a tattered volume of *Pilgrim's Progress*.

"Not that!" snapped the exasperated captain. "I want to see one of those calfskin-bound books."

As he pulled out Edwards' *Sermons*, Sam's hands trembled so violently that he almost dropped the weighty tome on Captain Lynnwood's head. The captain reached up impatiently to snatch the book. He carried it over to a window to thumb through the pages. "Very interesting," he murmured. "I've heard that this Edwards was a preacher of great power."

"Yes. And he certainly wouldn't approve of what you're up to!" Sam muttered under his breath.

The captain swung around to face him. "What was that? We'll have no insolence! Now hand me the rest of those books!"

As Sam took the next volume from the shelf, his heart gave a great leap. Behind it was a fat, solid-looking red book — just the sort of book to hold a fortune in gold! Unfortunately, Captain Lynnwood had seen it also and his curiosity was aroused.

"Let me see that red book!" he commanded.

Sam gritted his teeth. Should he grab the "gold books," jump off the ladder, and bolt out of the room? The books would be a heavy load to carry and the young officers were playing cards downstairs. If Captain Lynnwood shouted an alarm, he'd never make it out of the house. He wondered wildly if he should hit the captain with one of the books and try to knock him out.

"Wake up, you dull-witted clod!" roared the captain. "'Pon my word, I think you take pleasure in annoying me."

"Captain Lynnwood!" called Colonel Watts from the next room.

Sam gasped in thankfulness at the interruption.

The captain stepped into the hall, where he met the portly colonel coming from his room. Colonel Watts was dressed to go out. He was limping painfully and leaning on a gold-headed cane.

"I'll trouble you for your arm downstairs to my sleigh, Captain," he groaned. "I'd not venture out this cold day had not General Howe summoned me to an important council."

"Wait there, boy!" the captain called over his shoulder. The two officers started a slow walk along the hall and down the stairs.

In the library, Sam shoved the Edwards books aside and pawed with frantic haste at the two fat red books on the shelf behind them. Eagerly he dragged one off the shelf. Its weight left no doubt that it was one of the treasure books. Clutching it to his chest, he backed down the ladder and put the book on the floor. He swarmed back up the ladder to get the second book. Stooped over with the weight of the two books as he gripped them in his arms, he stared around like a cornered animal. There was no safe hiding place in the library, yet he must be quick to get the books out of sight.

He stole heavily out of the library and into Colonel Watts' room. If he could find a hiding place here, he could pretend to come up and mend the fire before the colonel returned and then smuggle the books downstairs in the woodbasket. The storeroom downstairs was as safe a place to keep them as he could think of, and tonight he'd take them to Mr. Clay.

He pulled open the door of the mahogany wardrobe and peered at the row of uniforms and polished boots ranged beneath them. No place to hide books in there. But wait — the blanket chest! Sam closed the wardrobe door and turned to the cedar chest that stood beneath a window. He lifted the lid, burrowed into the extra quilts and blankets that were kept there, and hid the books at the bottom of the pile.

When Captain Lynnwood returned to the library, Sam was sitting innocently on the ladder.

"Now hand me down that book!" the captain said briskly.

Sam instantly reached down a book that he had planted on the shelf. It was the same color and size as the "gold books." The captain examined it and then handed it back with a scowl of disappointment. "Just a book of local history," he said with a shrug.

For the rest of the afternoon Sam toiled quite cheerfully packing books. By the time he had finished this task, Colonel Watts had returned home and gone to bed, stating that he must have his dinner brought up to him. Sam would have no opportunity to get into the bedroom by himself again that day. But the "gold books" were well hidden. Tomorrow he would surely find a way to get them out of the house.

Caught!

TOMORROW was the day of Captain Lynn-wood's farewell party and Sam was kept busy in the kitchen, peeling potatoes and turning a huge roast of beef upon the fireside spit. Ellen arrived early to help Mrs. Andrews make pies. They sliced a ham and arranged the meat on platters, then they took turns whipping a huge bowl of thick cream for a syllabub.* Sam cracked walnuts and polished apples, then went into the dining room to set out the dishes for caraway comfits, almond cookies, and little cakes.

When the dinner hour drew near, Mr. Andrews, stately in his white wig, with ruffled linen at his throat and cuffs and silver buckles to his shoes, stationed himself in the candlelit hall to open the door for the guests. They came in sleighs and sedan chairs, British offi-

* a sweet dessert

143

cers with powdered hair, wearing gold-braided uniforms beneath their swirling cloaks, rich Tories in velvet with gold-embroidered waistcoats, British ladies and Tory belles in bouffant gowns of satin and brocade, with jewels and flowers in their powdered curls. Ellen watched them eagerly through a crack in the kitchen door.

"Look, Sam, how the diamonds sparkle in the candlelight," she whispered. "And there's a lady with an amethyst necklace."

"I don't want to look," Sam said crossly. "Seeing those strutting popinjays reminds me that there aren't enough blankets to go around at Valley Forge, and it's a rare Continental soldier who has a whole seat to his breeches."

Ellen gave him a stricken look and turned away from the door. Two teardrops rolled down her cheeks.

"For shame, Sam Woodbury!" Mrs. Andrews scolded. "Why couldn't you let the maid admire the fine clothes, if it gives her pleasure? 'Twill not clothe a single Continental soldier if she refuses to look at the British dandies."

Sam's heart smote him when he saw Ellen's tears. By way of saying that he was sorry, he snitched a fragrant pink rose from the centerpiece on the dining table and went back to the kitchen to thrust it into Ellen's hand. She brushed away her tears with a corner of her apron and smiled at him as she fastened the rose to her dress.

"The gold we're going to take home tonight will buy lots of blankets, food, and medicine for the men at Valley Forge," he whispered.

Sam, spruced up in a suit that Mr. Andrews had found for him, and Ellen, pretty in her blue frock and ruffled white apron, helped Mr. Andrews with the serving. Sam was thankful that Major and Mrs. Darcy were not among the guests, for the major would certainly have asked what Ellen and he were doing in that house. As it was, no one except Lieutenant Carvel paid them the slightest attention, and to him Ellen whispered that Mrs. Andrews had asked her to help.

Once the dinner was served, their work was over for awhile. Mr. Andrews stayed on duty in the dining room. Mrs. Andrews was asleep in her kitchen armchair.

"Now is my time to go upstairs," Sam murmured to Ellen. "I'll drop the gold books into the snow beneath the colonel's window. We'll pick them up when I walk you home."

"Oh, Sam, be careful!"

He squeezed her hand and then went softly up the back stairs. In the upper hall, he leaned over the balustrade to make sure that no one was coming up the front stairs. The hall was deserted. Sounds of conversation and ripples of laughter came from the dining room, where the glittering company was still gathered around the candlelit table. Sam stole along to the colonel's room.

The big room with its curtained bed was dimly lighted by two candles set in silver candlesticks at either end of the fireplace mantel. Red shadows from the logs glowing on the hearth danced on the walls. Sam rushed over to the blanket chest and opened the window above it. A draft of icy air swept into the room. Shivering more from nervousness than from cold, Sam opened the chest and felt beneath the bedding. With a grunt of satisfaction he brought out the books. He let the lid of the chest down softly and dropped the books out of the window, leaning far out to watch them sink into the big snowdrift below.

An overwhelming feeling of relief came to him as he closed the window. At last the books were out of this house! The rest should be easy.

He started toward the door. Almost under his foot, something bright glinted in the firelight. He stopped and picked up a gold pin set with rubies, a pin such as gentlemen used to decorate the lace ruffles they wore at their throats. He was standing with the pin in his hand when the door opened. Captain Lynnwood and Colonel Watts came into the room. The colonel was limping and the captain was helping him along.

"I was sorry to leave our merry company," Colonel Watts was saying. "But my gout is very painful tonight." He paused in surprise when he saw Sam.

"What are you doing here, boy?" Captain Lynnwood demanded.

Suddenly Sam's mind seemed to become a blank. For the life of him he couldn't think of a good excuse for being in the colonel's room. A lump swelled in his throat. He stammered something about mending the fire, then looked miserably guilty because the logs in the fireplace obviously hadn't been touched in a long time.

"What's that in your hand?" The captain reached out and snatched the ruby pin from Sam's fingers. "I believe that this is your property, sir."

"Why, yes." The colonel looked surprised and put his hand up to his lace ruffles. "I thought I had pinned it on." He took the pin and gave Sam a stern glance. "Where did you get this pin, Sam?"

"It was right here on the rug. I was going to put it on the lowboy."

"A likely story!" Captain Lynnwood jeered. "You meant to steal it."

Sam's eyes flashed. "That's not true!"

"I say that you came up here to do a little pilfering while the rest of us were downstairs."

Sam clenched his fists. "I'm not a thief."

But it was impossible to think of a good excuse for being in the colonel's room. If only he had thought to bring a warming pan from the kitchen! He stared defiantly at the two officers. Perhaps if they threw him into prison, Ellen would find a way to get the gold to her uncle.

"What else did you take? Turn out your pockets!" Captain Lynnwood ordered.

"I didn't take anything."

"We'll see about that."

The captain grabbed Sam by the collar and began to paw at the pockets of his breeches. Sam struggled and twisted and finally succeeded in tearing away. Then he himself turned his pockets inside out. "You see?" he said to the colonel.

"Only because we surprised you before you had time to take anything but the ruby pin," said Captain Lynnwood.

Sam went white with fury. "You're a fine one to talk about thieves," he exploded. "If

you're not stealing Mr. Milton's books I'd like
to know what you call it."

"Why you — you young — " The captain
choked on his anger. He grabbed the colonel's
cane and brought it down hard across Sam's
shoulders. Sam dodged away before another
blow could reach him; then the colonel spoke
sharply. "Have done, Captain Lynnwood."

The captain reluctantly lowered the cane.
Colonel Watts sank into an easy chair.

"Why did you turn thief, Sam?" he asked.
His voice and expression were patient and
kindly. "I know that there is much poverty and
hardship among the poor of Philadelphia this
winter. If you are desperate to obtain money to
buy food or firewood for your family, I could
forgive you and even help you."

Sam was surprised and touched, but he
wasn't going to confess to a crime he hadn't
committed.

"I'm not a thief," he repeated through set
lips.

"Why waste time with this rascal?" Captain
Lynnwood put in impatiently. "I'll call the
guard and have him taken to jail!"

"No, I refuse to be responsible for sending
a boy to prison." The colonel's tone was firm.
"Nor will I permit a thief to stay under my
roof," he added with a stern look at Sam.

Sam writhed at the hateful word.

"Sam, if I show you mercy, will you promise to mend your ways?" Without waiting for an answer, the colonel dug into the pocket of his white satin breeches and brought out a handful of silver. "Take this, Sam."

Sam backed away. "I don't want your money."

"Nonsense." The colonel stood up and thrust the money into Sam's unwilling hand. "Begone now, before Captain Lynnwood persuades me to change my mind about the jail. And follow honest ways in the future."

"I wasn't going to steal the pin!" Sam repeated stubbornly.

Captain Lynnwood snorted.

"If you wish to thank me for being lenient toward you, join me in saying 'God save the King,' " the colonel said.

Sam stiffened. *Here I go!* he thought. But no matter what happened to him, he wasn't going to deny his country! He stood taller. "I can't say that, sir. My watchword is 'God save our Country'!"

The colonel's heavy face turned scarlet.

"You see?" Captain Lynnwood said triumphantly. "There's no good in the young scamp at all."

"I fear that you are right." Colonel Watts looked so angry that Sam trembled with fear of being marched off immediately to the dismal British prison. Then the colonel waved a hand in dismissal. "A thief and a traitor to your King. If you were older, I'd make an example of you. Now go! And never let me see you again."

Sam opened his hand and let the colonel's silver spill to the floor, then he tore out of the room and down the stairs. He had discovered that in serving one's country the bravest deeds are not always performed upon the battlefield. As long as he lived he'd never forget the scorn on the faces of those enemy officers as they called him "thief."

In the kitchen, Mrs. Andrews and Ellen were doing the dinner dishes. Mr. Andrews was sitting wearily before the fire. He looked up, startled, when Sam burst into the room.

"Is something wrong, Sam?" he asked anxiously.

"Something's terribly wrong!"

Ellen swung around, holding a silver platter in one hand and a dish towel in the other. "Sam, did you get the — "

"Shh!" Sam told her fiercely. He turned to Mr. Andrews. "Colonel Watts has ordered me out of the house."

All three of them stared at him in astonishment and dismay. Sam didn't have time to explain. He didn't dare delay a moment in getting the treasure books out of the snowdrift.

"I must go at once. They'll tell you that I'm a thief," he warned them miserably.

Mr. Andrews stood up and put a fatherly hand on Sam's shoulder. "I'm not asking any questions," he said quietly. "I know that you were sent here by Mr. Milton on our country's business and that's enough for me. We know that you are no thief, Sam."

Sam gripped his hand gratefully. "Someday I'll be able to tell you the whole story. Until then, thanks for believing in me."

While Sam was shrugging into his jacket, Mr. Andrews took Ellen's cloak from its wall peg and flung it around her shoulders. "You'd both best get away from here before someone comes to see if Sam has really left the house," he said.

As Sam followed Ellen out into the frosty night, he drew in a deep breath of cold air. It was like being let out of prison. He pulled Ellen into the shadow of the high box hedge. "Wait here for me," he whispered.

She nodded. "But hurry!" In the shadow of her hood her eyes looked big and frightened.

Sam hunched over to make himself small and kept as much as possible in the shadow of trees and shrubs as he made his way along the snowy garden path. He worried about the tracks he was making. But overhead, clouds were scudding across the stars and the wind had a sharp nip that held promise of a storm. Perhaps by morning new snow would have covered his footprints.

From behind the brocade curtains of the drawing-room windows came the sound of music and voices. Across a snow-frosted stretch of lawn Sam could see a British soldier stamping up and down before the front door of the house with his musket over his shoulder. Coachmen who had brought guests were walking blanketed horses, unhitched from the sleighs, up and down the driveway. Near the gate, some chair carriers were warming themselves at a blazing fire that they had kindled in the snow. Probably they were burning the fences of patriotic citizens, Sam thought gloomily.

He crouched behind a bush. None of the people in the drive were looking in his direction, so he ran to the drift beneath the colonel's window and burrowed into it like a squirrel searching for a store of nuts. He grunted with satisfaction when his mittened hands touched the books. Then he had them clutched tightly against him and was creeping back to where Ellen was waiting.

"Oh, Sam, you've got them!" Ellen sounded as if she hadn't really believed in the "gold books" until now. "Let me carry one of them."

She pulled one of the books away from Sam but it was so unexpectedly heavy that she dropped it. Sam picked it up with a grin. "Gold is heavy, you know."

"I'll manage." Ellen hid the book under her cloak.

Sam looked cautiously up and down the street. The houses along here were widely spaced, but light from the fire near the Milton driveway was flickering on the road. Sam dared not walk past that fire and risk being questioned by the sentry, even though turning in the opposite direction meant a much longer walk to the Clay house. He tugged at Ellen's cloak. "Come on. But don't hurry. We don't want it to look as if we were ruuning away."

The night was so cold and windy that they met few people, even when they neared the center of the city. They were still a few blocks from home when they met the Watch, striding along with his lantern and staff. He paused and held the lantern high as he peered into the two young faces, glowing with cold.

" 'Tis past curfew time," he reminded them sternly. He squinted more closely at Ellen. "Are you Seth Clay's niece?"

"Yes, sir," Ellen answered faintly. Under her cloak her arms hugged the heavy book tightly.

"And who may you be?" the Watch demanded of Sam. "Why are the two of ye on the streets at this hour?"

Two British soldiers came out of a tavern across the street and paused to stare at the Watch and the two young people. The Watch shook his staff at them.

"Get along with you! No loitering on the streets!" he shouted.

The soldiers tramped away toward the barracks without giving him any argument. The Watch turned back to Sam.

"Now, young fellow, what's your name?"

"Sam Woodbury, sir. I work for Mr. Clay and I'm walking Ellen home. She's been visiting friends."

"You seem an honest chap," the Watch admitted. "But take care not to be out so late another time." He strolled on, his lantern a glowing star in the winter darkness.

Sam and Ellen hurried on their way. They were almost home now.

The bookshop was dark. Curtains were drawn across the windows of the Clay house, but candlelight flickered inside. Sam tapped the front-door knocker softly. In a minute Mr.

Clay flung the door wide and pulled him and Ellen into the hall.

"We've got it!" Sam whooped, as soon as the door was closed.

Mr. Clay herded them into the parlor, where Mrs. Clay and he had been waiting anxiously. Ellen's mother gave a cry of joy at the sight of them. She hugged Ellen and then Sam. George jumped down from the sofa and rubbed against Sam, purring a welcome.

With a thump Ellen dropped her book on the floor. "Open it, Uncle Seth. Let's see if there's gold in there or iron bolts."

Mrs. Clay spread her shawl on the table and all of them gathered around while Mr. Clay used a kitchen knife to pry up the glued covers of the books. The pages had been cut away, leaving only a thin, strong outer wall, and the hollow was filled with gold pieces. Golden guineas! Spanish dollars gleamed richly in the candlelight. Mr. Clay poured them out in a stream upon his sister-in-law's shawl.

"Ahh — " Sam murmured. Instead of gold, he was seeing blankets, food, and medicine that this money would buy for the ragged army at Valley Forge.

A week passed. Every day Sam and the Clay family waited anxiously for George Brooks to appear at the Sign of the Red Goose Quill and claim General Washington's gold. Mr. Clay had transferred the gold pieces to two stout canvas bags and had hidden them in a corner of the woodbox in the bookshop. Sam kept the box heaped high with logs and kindling, so that no chance glance from an enemy officer would discover the hidden bags. The responsibility and danger of having the treasure on the premises kept the whole family on edge. Still George Brooks did not come.

One night a furtive knock sounded on the kitchen door. When Sam answered it, he was amazed to see the watchman who had stopped Ellen and him on the street. Tonight he was not carrying his official staff and lantern and his hat was tipped to hide his face.

The man refused to come in. Standing on the doorstep, he spoke in a mumble so low that Sam was obliged to bend close to understand him. "Tell Seth Clay that Brooks was seized by the British today, while he was trying to pass the barrier into town. They've flung him into prison on the pretext that his pass was not in order."

"Oh!" Sam groaned. "That's the worst thing that could possibly happen."

The watchman's sharp eyes looked deep into his for a moment. "God save our country!" he whispered.

Before Sam could recover from his surprise, the man had disappeared into the shadows. Sam stared after him thrilled and astounded. The Watch was a Patriot, one of the courageous people who dared to serve their country in the very presence of the enemy!

"Who was that?" Mr. Clay asked, as Sam closed the door.

"A friend," Sam said with a meaningful glance. "But he brought bad news. George Brooks was arrested as he was coming into the city this morning."

Ellen, her mother, and Mr. Clay all uttered cries of dismay.

"He was on his way to pick up the gold," Mr. Clay said, shaking his head.

"Will they hang him?" Ellen asked anxiously.

"I fear that they will," was her uncle's grim reply. "That is a fate that we who serve our country as secret agents must be prepared to meet."

He began to pace up and down the room, his forehead creased by a frown. "The British too have their spies and one of them must have discovered something that betrayed poor Brooks. This may well mean the end of the usefulness of the bookshop as a link in the chain of General Washington's intelligence," he muttered. "Major Darcy may remember that he saw Brooks at the Sign of the Red Goose Quill, and in that case we too will be under suspicion and American agents will no longer dare stop here to pick up news."

Sam noted with pride that the bookseller seemed little worried about any danger to himself, but was concerned only because he feared that he could no longer be of service to General Washington.

The Snowball Fight

MAJOR Darcy did indeed remember where he had seen Brooks. The next morning he walked into the bookshop and put Mr. Clay through an uncomfortable hour while he questioned him about his relations with the suspected spy. He went away at last without having forced any important information out of the shrewd bookseller.

Sam had the jitters all the while the British officer was in the shop, standing near the woodbox.

"What are we going to do about that gold?" he demanded, when he and Mr. Clay were alone.

"We'll have to keep it until our people find some way to get it out to Valley Forge."

"But our men need it *now!*" Sam said. He kicked at the woodbox, angered by his own helplessness in the matter.

The next afternoon Sam walked across town to deliver a book to a customer. On his way home, he was surprised to see a squad of British soldiers turning from Fourth Street into Arch, where they entered a house without the formality of asking permission. A smart young lieutenant was in command of the squad, but Major Darcy was there also, and the major was wearing a grim, determined expression. Sam pushed into the crowd of people who had gathered to watch the Redcoats and found himself standing next to Carter Greene, a schoolmate who was as ardent a Patriot as Sam himself.

"What's going on?" Sam asked.

"That spy they caught has escaped from prison."

Sam bit his lip to hold back a cheer. "Did he get clean away?"

Carter shook his head. "Some lobsterback saw him heading this way, but at the time he didn't know that Brooks was an escaped prisoner. Later, the soldier learned of the escape and was given Brooks' description, but by then Brooks had disappeared. The British are searching every house in this part of town. They know that Brooks couldn't get very far in this weather, because he's wearing only his shirt and breeches."

"See you — " Sam muttered.

He elbowed his way through the crowd and

ran all the way to Sassafras Lane, where he burst into the shop.

"Not so boisterous!" Mr. Clay reproved. He went on serving a customer.

Sam pretended to busy himself rearranging some books on a table, but he thought he'd burst with the news churning inside him before the lady finally made her purchase and left the shop.

"Mr. Clay!" Sam gasped, as the door closed behind the departing customer. "George Brooks has escaped from prison!"

Mr. Clay looked at him with a grim smile.

"You knew!" Sam exclaimed. When the bookseller nodded, he asked in a hoarse whisper, "Did he come here?"

"Of course. We are his friends."

Sam grabbed the older man's arm. "But the Redcoats are searching all the houses in this neighborhood. Soon they'll be on Sassafras Lane, and Major Darcy is with them!"

Mr. Clay was as calm as Sam was excited. "Brooks won't be here when they arrive. He's in the office now, putting on some clothes I gave him. He'll walk out of this shop as if he were a customer and then go to the house of a Patriot who has a secret room under his woodshed. This man will hide Brooks until he finds a way of getting him safely out of the city."

The bookseller glanced out of the window. Blue shadows were deepening in the snowy street. Soon it would be dusk. "Light the candles, Sam," he said. "It will look suspicious if we don't show some light. And get the gold out of the woodbox. Brooks will take it with him.

He went into the office to hurry his dangerous visitor.

Sam lighted a long tallow dip and stepped outside to touch it to the candles in the lanterns; then he hurried back to light the candles in the sconces. Finally he dug into the woodbox and pulled out the canvas bags of gold. Not daring to stand there with a bag of gold in each hand, he pulled up his ample homespun shirt and bundled the bags underneath, holding them in place with his arms clutched across his middle, since his jacket wouldn't button over the bulge. He would hand the bags to George Brooks as the man was going out the door.

Ellen came running from the house with her face white with terror. Her uncle had set her to watching the lane from the parlor windows. "The soldiers are on this street!" she cried.

"Tell Brooks to hurry!" Sam yelped.

As Ellen flew to the office, Sam stepped outside for a look at the situation. There were no soldiers to be seen, but the crowd of angry men and boys who had followed Major Darcy's squad was large enough to choke the lane.

In the shop, Mr. Clay had come out of the office, followed by George Brooks. The American intelligence agent was wearing one of Mr. Clay's powdered wigs, a tricorn hat, and a long black cloak with one end thrown over his shoulder, so that it partly hid his face. The two men hurried to the door, but just as Brooks was about to step outside, a soldier popped out of the house two doors away and shouted at the crowd, ordering the people to go home. He made a threatening pass with the bayonet fixed to his musket to back up his command.

The crowd fell back sullenly but did not break up. Carter Greene gave a catcall that was echoed by the other boys. The soldier rushed at them threateningly with his bayonet, and they drew back as far as the bookshop. Taunts of "Tyrants!" and "Lobsterbacks!" rent the dusk.

"Now!" Mr. Clay said to Brooks, as the people surged back to the bookshop door.

George Brooks stepped out boldly, and Sam, suddenly remembering the gold under his shirt, whipped out the bags and started to hand them to him; but just then Major Darcy, angered by the disturbance in the street, strode out of the house that was being searched. The tall figure of George Brooks was outlined by the lights at the bookshop door and the major's quick eyes saw him at once and narrowed with suspicion.

"You there!" he shouted. "Stand in the name of the King!"

Brooks dashed into the crowd, which opened to let him through and then closed up again. Sam could see him legging it along the lane behind the mass of people. But the soldiers would scatter the crowd with their bayonets and be after him. He must have time to get away!

The other soldiers of the squad were pouring into the lane. Helpless himself because he had to hang on to the gold, Sam shouldered his way to where Carter and his friends were shouting insults at the enemy.

"Snowballs make better weapons than words!" he hinted.

"Whoops!" Carter yelled with enthusiasm. "Come on, boys! Up and at 'em!"

He scooped a handful of slushy snow out of the street and squeezed it into a hard ball which he let fly at Major Darcy. The snowball missed the major but knocked off the hat of a soldier just behind him. Suddenly the air was full of snowballs and the boys hit their targets hard enough and often enough to throw the enemy into confusion. But the soldiers soon recovered. Roaring with fury as the snow smashed against their heads and faces, they charged the crowd with their bayonets.

The crowd scattered before the sharp steel and carried Sam with it along the lane. George Brooks had disappeared in the darkness. As he panted along with his burden of gold, Sam glanced back over his shoulder. The angry major had called his men back and now the squad was drawn up in front of the bookshop. No going back there with General Washington's gold.

People were melting into the shadows of backyards and alleys, leaving the enemy in possession of Sassafras Lane. Following two other boys, Sam raced along a dark and slippery alley. The boys disappeared into a house. Sam found himself at a dead end with a high board fence ahead of him and the sound of British soldiers, now reorganized into an efficient searching party, coming along Sassafras Lane.

He was well acquainted with this part of Philadelphia. There was a livery stable behind the fence with British Army horses quartered in it. There were bound to be soldiers at the stable, but he had no choice of which direction he must take. He heaved the bags of gold over the fence and then scrambled after them, dropping into a narrow space between the fence and the back of the stable. He crouched, listening.

Voices shouting commands echoed from Sassafras Lane. Two soldiers were tramping along the alley. One poked into a woodshed with the point of his bayonet. The other leaped to grab hold of the top of the fence and hoist himself up so he could see over it. Sam flattened out in the snow and held his breath, thankful for the shadow cast by the stable. The soldier took only a quick look along the rear of the stable. He was looking for a man, not a boy, and evidently he decided that a big man like the American spy could never have wedged himself into the narrow space between the fence and stable. He dropped back into the alley and rejoined his companion, who was pounding on a door. Windows were opened and heads appeared. Voices demanded to know what was wanted.

"Open up!" bawled the Redcoat. "We're looking for an escaped prisoner."

While the search continued, Sam huddled in the snow, shivering with cold, and frantic to get the gold to a safe place. His feet felt numb. Soon he would be too cramped from the cold to move. Would the search never end?

Suddenly aware that his head was nodding, he got to his feet and stamped in the snow. He wriggled his cold toes inside his wet brogans and rubbed his hands together. The night was so cold that his breath hung in the air like a mist of ice crystals. He must start moving!

Where could he go? Not back to the bookshop. Now that the escaped prisoner had been seen coming out of the Sign of the Red Goose Quill, Mr. Clay would be suspected by the British and might even be taken to the prison. The Clay house and shop were no longer safe hiding places for the gold.

It occurred to Sam that the only people in Philadelphia whom he dared trust with the dangerous secret of the gold were Mr. and Mrs. Andrews. He would ask them to hide it until some plan could be made to get it out of the city. He smiled grimly as, with the two heavy bags clutched tightly in one arm and hand, he made his way cautiously along in the drifts between the stable and the fence. After all the peril of getting the gold away from the Milton house, he was now on his way to take it back there!

Rounding the stable wall with caution, he found himself in the open space between the stable and a carriage house which had been turned into living quarters for the soldiers who took care of the horses. Lanterns cast a yellow glow on the doors of house and stable, but there were no soldiers loitering outside in the cold. Sam darted across the cobblestones of the stable yard and out into the alley on which the stable fronted. He ran along the shadowy alley until he came to a wider street of houses and shops. He stepped boldly into the street and started walking at an ordinary pace toward the Milton house.

It was quite late when he found himself in the shadow of the hedge at Mr. Milton's kitchen door. Candlelight glimmering through the frosted windowpanes told him that Mr. and Mrs. Andrews were still downstairs, but because of the thick frost he couldn't see inside. He'd have to take a chance.

He knocked sharply at the windowpane, waited a second, and knocked again. He was poised for a flight. If anyone but Mr. Andrews answered his knock, he'd be off as fast as his legs would carry him.

The house door opened and Mr. Andrews' head, covered by a nightcap, popped out. He started when he saw Sam.

"Is it safe for me to come in?" Sam asked hoarsely.

Without a word, Mr. Andrews reached out, clutched Sam's sleeve, and dragged him into the kitchen, closing and barring the door behind him.

Mrs. Andrews, in her wrapper and nightcap, was sitting on the fireside settle with a mug of hot chocolate in her hand. At the sight of Sam, she started violently.

"Land sakes!" she exclaimed. "What are *you* doing here?"

"Shhh!" Sam implored in a low voice. He glanced nervously at the door leading to the front hall.

"All the officers are at General Howe's ball," said Mr. Andrews. Sam heaved a sigh of relief, dropped the bags of gold on the settle, and blurted out his story. The couple listened in amazement. This was the first that they had heard of Mr. Milton's treasure.

"To think that you got that gold out of the house right under the noses of the British!" Mrs. Andrews exclaimed in wonder. "But you could have trusted us, Sam."

"The fewer people knowing such a dangerous secret the better," her husband reminded her.

"Will you hide the gold until General Washington can send someone to get it?" Sam asked.

Mr. Andrews shook his head. "It wouldn't be safe for one of the General's agents to come here. We have a new officer living here, and Colonel Watts has a new orderly who sleeps in the library. He's a nosy fellow, always poking about, and he'd be likely to see and question anyone who came to the door. Luckily, he too is away tonight."

"Did Colonel Watts make any trouble for you on my account?" Sam asked worriedly.

"No. He simply told me not to hire anyone else." Mr. Andrews stroked his chin thoughtfully. "Sam, you're the one who will have to take the gold to Valley Forge," he decided.

"I?" Sam yelped. "But I couldn't get past the British lines."

"We'll find a way to get you out of the city, and until we do, we'll hide you here."

The Road to Valley Forge

SAM gulped as he considered this new plan. "Colonel Watts warned me never to let him set eyes on me again," he reminded Mr. Andrews.

"The colonel won't suspect that you are here. We'll make you a bed in the storeroom next to our bedroom. No one ever goes there. Daytimes, you can warm yourself before the fire in our room."

Mrs. Andrews nodded, then she got to her feet. "I'll fix you a bite to eat before we tuck you in."

Sam ate a hearty meal of roast chicken, bread and butter, and a mug of chocolate. Afterward, he followed his friends up the narrow back stairs by the dim light of the candle carried by Mr. Andrews. After they had left him, wrapped in a cocoon of quilts and blankets on the floor of the cold, dark little attic room, his thoughts at last had time to go to Ellen and her uncle. He wondered anxiously how they had fared in the face of Major Darcy's suspicion and anger. By this time they had probably discovered that the gold was gone from the woodbox. Would they link its disappearance with the fact that Sam hadn't come home? Sam's hand went out to touch the chunky bags. *Tomorrow,* he thought tiredly, as he snuggled down in his quilts, *maybe Mr. Andrews can get word to Mr. Clay that the gold is safe.*

Sam was ravenously hungry by the time that Mr. Andrews was able to smuggle him some dinner the next day. Mr. Andrews had been to market and there he had asked questions of people he knew to be Patriots. He brought Sam the good word that George Brooks had not been recaptured.

"And by this time he is hidden safely away somewhere. But the news about Mr. Clay is not so good. Major Darcy blames him for Brooks' escape, even though he has no evidence against him except that a man resembling Brooks was seen coming out of the bookshop. The British have thrown Mr. Clay into prison and closed the bookshop."

Sam lost his appetite for his dinner. "What will Ellen and her mother do with no way to earn a living?"

"As soon as the excitement over Brooks dies

down, I'll get in touch with Mrs. Clay and try to help her," Mr. Andrews promised. "I dare not go there now."

"Tell them what happened to me," Sam said soberly. "I don't want them thinking that I deserted them when they needed me."

The days passed slowly for Sam in his attic hidey-hole. Mr. Andrews kept a warm fire going in the bedroom fireplace and Sam sat before it daytimes, but he had to be careful about moving about, lest footsteps in the attic, while the Andrews were downstairs, alert the Colonel's orderly to go up there and investigate.

Sam worried a lot about Ellen and her family and finally the idea came to him that Mr. Clay's friend, the Town Watch, might have some news of them. Mr. Andrews managed to meet this man one night, while he was on his rounds. Not daring to engage him in conversation, he paused only long enough to slip him a purse with a little money in it for Mrs. Clay, and to ask the Watch to pass the word to Ellen to meet Mr. Andrews at the Town Market the next day.

Ellen was at the market when Mr. Andrews arrived to do his lavish shopping for Colonel Watts' table. She had a few carrots in her basket and was looking over a pile of turnips.

174

Mr. Andrews bought a plump fowl and managed to slip it into her basket without anyone else noticing what he was about. He dared not speak openly to Ellen. She could be watched by British agents, in the hope that she might lead them to Sam or Brooks. Mr. Andrews stood beside her pretending to choose a turnip, and whispered that both Sam and something he had were safe. Soon Sam would be going to the country, Mr. Andrews whispered, hoping Ellen would realize he meant Valley Forge.

Later, Mr. Andrew met the Watch again, and the man told him that Mrs. Clay was allowed to visit her brother-in-law at the prison and take him food. This was because old Mr. Stone, of all people, had interceded with General Howe on behalf of his neighbors, and Mr. Stone was in high favor with the British.

When Sam heard this, he mentally took back some of the hard thoughts he had about Mr. Stone.

"It seems," Mr. Andrews continued with a smile, "Mr. Stone told General Howe that if anyone at the bookshop had a hand in helping Brooks escape it was a certain young firebrand named Sam Woodbury."

Sam stared at him and then began to laugh.

"Because your master, James Leeds, is such a red-hot Patriot, Mr. Stone persuaded the

British that he was probably an agent for General Washington also and that you took over for him when he was forced to leave town."

"That's fine with me if it takes the blame off Mr. Clay," Sam said jauntily. Then he clenched his fists over his own helplessness at this time when Ellen and her mother needed friends.

Mr. Andrews gave him an understanding glance. "Ellen sent word to you not to worry about her," he said. "But to get yourself and 'you-know-what' safely out of Philadelphia. They'll be waiting for you at the Sign of the Red Goose Quill when you return with General Washington in the spring."

It was Mrs. Andrews who came up with a plan for getting Sam out of the city.

"Colonel Watts has promised us a pass for Molly, our granddaughter, so that she can visit her cousins in the country. Molly is about your age, and as she has never come here since the British moved into the house, Colonel Watts won't know if you use the pass instead of her."

"But the pass will be made out to a girl," Sam reminded her.

"So you'll have to play the part of Molly during your walk past the British sentries."

"You want me to walk out of Philadelphia wearing girls' clothes?" Sam cried, outraged.

"It's the only way you can get through the lines. And I declare, Sam, you'll make a pretty girl," Mrs. Andrews said with a chuckle.

"I won't do it!" Sam folded his arms and thrust out his lip.

"Don't you want General Washington to get the gold? Is your pride greater than your desire to help our soldiers?"

Sam stared down unhappily at his shabby shoes. Some of the men at Valley Forge didn't have *any* shoes! "I'll use Molly's pass," he muttered.

Since Molly's clothes were too small for Sam, Mrs. Andrews set busily about preparing something for him to wear. She quilted the gold pieces into a red flannel petticoat, and she made him a dress out of an old blue woolen one of her own. From a chest, in the attic, she brought out a warm, dark-blue cloak belonging to Mr. Milton. She shortened it for Sam and used one of the double capes to make a hood. Sam watched these preparations with sour looks.

At last the morning for his departure arrived. Mr. Andrews had chosen a day when all the officers in the house were away for an early inspection of the troops. Sam was jittery with suspense.

"Take your hair out of the club, Sam," Mrs. Andrews directed.

Sam untied the string that held back his sandy thatch, but when he saw Mrs. Andrews start to heat her curling iron on its little stand in the fireplace, he gave a yelp of protest. "You're not going to frizz my hair!"

"Sam, I must. All girls wear their hair in curls." She pushed the protesting boy into a chair. "I'll curl it just enough to show beneath the ruffle of your mobcap."

"Mobcap!" Sam howled.

"Sit still or I'll burn your ears." The smell of the hot iron on hair filled the room as Mrs. Andrews deftly made a frame of curls for Sam's face. Sam gritted his teeth and hunched his shoulders in misery. He would rather have crawled all the way to Valley Forge, dragging the gold bags in his teeth.

"Don't look so tragic," said Mrs. Andrews. "Lots of men curl their hair. The British officers in this house — "

"I don't care if King George curls his hair with a diamond poker!" Sam growled.

When the time came for him to put on the gold-heavy petticoat and the blue dress, he insisted upon wearing his breeches and jacket underneath.

"There aren't enough men's clothes to go around at Valley Forge," he reminded Mrs. Andrews. "And I'm not going through the rest of the winter dressed like a girl."

She sighed but gave in. "With all those things underneath, you make a fat girl," she gasped, as she struggled to button Sam's dress up the back. "Don't take a deep breath or you'll burst your buttons. Maybe I should lace you into a pair of my stays," she teased.

"Oh, no, you don't!" Sam backed away in alarm.

She laughed and set the frilled mobcap on his head, pulling the curled locks out around his forehead and cheeks. Sam took one look at himself in the mirror above the lowboy and wished that he could curl up like a porcupine.

"Don't scowl so," Mrs. Andrews begged. "Smile if you have to talk to British soldiers at the barrier, and flutter your eyelashes. And mind that you keep you voice low and sweet."

Sam groaned.

Mrs. Andrews draped the cloak with its jaunty shoulder cape around him and pulled the hood over his cap. "You'll pass, I do believe," she said with a pleased smile. "But remember to take short steps."

Moving awkwardly as the heavy petticoat and blue gown swung against his legs, Sam followed Mrs. Andrews down to the kitchen. He dreaded the moment when he must leave the house. He was sure the first person he met would see through his disguise. Mrs. Andrews had packed some lunch in a basket, and she put some molasses candy, wrapped in a napkin, into the pocket of his cloak. "You can eat it as you go along. It's twenty miles to Valley Forge," she said worriedly. "And over snowy roads!"

"I'd think nothing of it if it weren't for these flapping petticoats." Now that it was time to go, Sam realized how fond he was of Mr. and Mrs. Andrews. "Thanks for everything," he said in a husky voice. "Molly is lucky to have you for a grandmother."

Tears came to her eyes. She hugged him and kissed his cheek. "Oh, Sam, be careful. God bring you safe to Valley Forge with the gold for our suffering soldiers."

Mr. Andrews was to accompany his "granddaughter" as far as the outer British lines. Sam tried to walk with a girl's short steps as he followed him out to the street, but there they paused in consternation. Colonel Watts' sleigh was gliding toward them, pulled by its prancy black horse. The colonel's orderly sat in front beside the driver, and the colonel was in the rear with a robe of beaver fur spread over his knees. When he saw Mr. Andrews, he called to the driver to stop. Then he beckoned Mr. Andrews over to the sleigh.

Sam's knees felt weak. *Here I go and the gold with me!* he thought, his heart racing and pounding against his ribs.

"Where are you going, Andrews?" asked the colonel.

"I'm taking my granddaughter to the outer lines." Mr. Andrews' voice was steady and natural.

"Ah, yes, I remember. This is the girl for whom I obtained the pass. Good morning, my dear."

Sam twisted his mouth into a shy smile and cast his eyes down modestly as he jerked an awkward curtsey. He expected the colonel to recognize him any moment now and let out a roar of rage. But surprisingly, the colonel said to Mr. Andrews, "My driver will take me to the house and then come back for you and Molly and drive you to the outer fort."

He waved his hand in friendly fashion as Mr. Andrews thanked him, and the sleigh whirled away to the front door of the house. When it returned, Mr. Andrews pushed Sam into the back seat and climbed in after him. They sped through the streets of Philadelphia with the silver sleigh bells a jingle.

Now that he had passed the first test of his disguise, relief and mirth bubbled inside Sam. He lolled back against the velvet cushions and pulled the fur robe over his knees.

"I didn't expect to ride out of town in such style, dear Grandpapa," he simpered.

"Don't get too smart," Mr. Andrews muttered. "You've still a long, perilous road to travel."

The British had built a string of forts across the strip of land between the Schuylkill and Delaware Rivers. The driver took his passengers as far as the outer picket in these fortifications and then waited for Mr. Andrews while the officer of the guard examined Molly's pass. The magic signature of General Howe made it possible for Sam to go on without any trouble.

Wishing to smooth the wintry journey for the young girl, the officer stepped over to a farm cart which had drawn up near the sleigh. "Do you go anywhere near the Curtis farm?" he asked.

"Within two miles of it," the farmer said.

"This girl is going there to visit relatives. I'd take it as a favor if you'd let her ride with you."

"Glad to. Hop up beside me, missy."

Sam shot Mr. Andrews a despairing glance, but he dared not refuse the invitation. Mr. Andrews helped him clamber into the cart and handed up the basket of food. Then he watched worriedly as the cart creaked away in the direction of Valley Forge.

Huddled beside the driver, Sam was in a ferment of worry. What if the man should drive him all the way to the Curtis farm? And what if the Curtis family should denounce him as an imposter traveling on Molly's pass? The farmer would surely haul him back to Philadelphia or turn him over to some roving troop of British dragoons or Tory raiders! He was tempted to jump out and take to his heels, but he realized that hampered as he was by his petticoats, the farmer would have little trouble in overtaking him.

Unaware of the thoughts that were tormenting his companion, the farmer seemed to be glad to have someone to talk to on the long drive. He told Sam that he had just delivered a load of farm produce at the British barracks.

"The King's forces pay for food in hard money, so it's worth my while to drive to the city, although I could save five miles by taking my food to Valley Forge. A man would be a fool to sell for worthless Continental paper money when he can get British gold and silver."

Sam gritted his teeth as rage boiled up in him. "Do all the farmers feel as you do?" he asked in a muffled voice.

"A few are crazy enough to take their stuff to Valley Forge." The farmer shrugged as if he were at a loss to understand such idiots. "But if word of what they're doing gets to the British, a scouting party of British or Tories is apt to swoop down on their farms and burn them out."

Sam took care to keep his face shadowed by his hood. "I've heard that there are Continental scouts also," he murmured.

The farmer nodded. "Allan McLane and Lighthorse Harry Lee make it hot for the British and Tories, when they can catch them."

The cart creaked on through woods and past farmhouses that looked bleak and lonely in the pale winter sunshine. They passed one house that was a charred ruin. Sam wondered gloomily if it had belonged to a Patriot family who had been burned out.

The farmer stopped his horse at a crossroads. "I'd take you all the way, missy, but I still have miles to go before reaching home and this old nag of mine is tired. The lane branching off to the Curtis farm is about two miles ahead."

"Thanks for bringing me this far." Eager to get away, Sam grasped his basket and jumped to the road, almost tripping over his petticoats. The farmer nodded and drove away, and Sam plodded on along the empty road.

It was good to be on his own, Sam thought as he strode along at as brisk a pace as possible in his bulky skirts. After he had passed the lane leading to the Curtis farm, he figured that he must be more than halfway to Valley

Forge. He covered another couple of miles and then began to look for a good place to eat lunch. He had passed another burned-out farm, and then on a hill set back from the road, a big stone farmhouse with smoke curling up from the chimneys. Sam had an uneasy feeling about how conspicuous he would look to anyone who might glance out of a farmhouse window. He decided that if he could find a good place to hide, he'd hole up and wait until dusk to continue his walk.

He came to where a road turned off into a stand of thick woods. Sam turned off with it. Big trees marched along on both sides of the road with thickets of glossy green laurel growing beneath them. The snow wasn't as deep as it was in the open. Perhaps he'd be able to find a dry place where he could rest awhile. He plunged in among the trees and pushed around a clump of laurel only to bring up short as a dark, thickset man stepped out from behind a bushy hemlock. Before Sam realized what was happening, one sinewy hand clumped down on his shoulder while the man's other hand was pressed over his mouth. His heart seemed to jump into his throat. He tried desperately to twist away from the steel-like grip.

"Girl make one little sound and lose scalp!" his captor warned in a whisper.

The man was wearing deerskin leggings and

shirt with a tattered blue blanket belted over them. A tomahawk was thrust into the belt. A cap of fox fur topped his shoulder-length straight black hair, and on his feet were fur-lined mocassins. For weapons, he had a bow and a quiver of arrows slung across his shoulder, a knife in his belt, and a rifle, which he had set against a rock when he stopped Sam. Sam couldn't believe his eyes. The man was certainly an Indian, but there hadn't been an Indian in this part of Pennsylvania for years and years.

"Let go of me!" he mumbled. "Who are you?"

The man ignored him. A second Indian had seemed to spring up from the forest floor. The first one pushed Sam toward him. "Take girl to captain," he ordered. "Quiet!" he warned Sam, patting his tomahawk.

The second Indian marched Sam around the thick hemlock. There they found a young man seated on a rock. Like the Indians, he was bronzed and sinewy and he wore a fringed buckskin hunting shirt. The rest of his costume included threadbare breeches and well-worn riding boots and a battered cocked hat. A sword and a brace of pistols hung from his belt. A look of astonishment crossed his handsome face when he saw Sam.

"Where did *you* come from, sis?" he asked pleasantly.

Sam was thankful for the hood that shaded his face. "Pray, sir, why did that Indian stop me?" he asked in his softest voice.

"Because this wood is no place for a girl right now." The young man stood up and bowed. "I am Allan McLane of the Continental Dragoons, at your service, miss."

Sam had to swallow an ungirl-like cheer. He had fallen among his own people! The exploits of gallant Allan McLane were a legend among Patriots.

"The Indians are Oneida, members of my troop of scouts," the captain explained. "Their tribe came in with us when the rest of the Six Nations of the Iroquois took the British side in the war. And now, sis," he added crisply, "since you've blundered into our midst, I'll have to detain you for a while. Some Tory raiders are due to come along this road soon with a convoy of wagons loaded with food for the Redcoats. Our fellows at Valley Forge need that food, and I intend to capture it for them."

He broke off as the scream of a bluejay sounded through the woods.

"There's the signal that the wagons are almost here. You get down behind this rock, sis, so you won't be hit by a stray bullet. Don't make a sound now! After this action is over, I'll set you free."

He walked away and disappeared in the direction of the road without giving Sam a chance to reply. Sam heaved a deep sigh as he looked after him. *Here I am dressed in girls' clothes,* he thought miserably, *while Captain McLane strikes a blow for our side.*

The captain hadn't given him a chance to explain that he wasn't Molly Andrews. Now that he thought about it, Sam decided that it would be too humiliating to reveal to the dashing dragoon and his Indian scouts that he was a boy togged out as a girl.

He stood tense and with his hands clenched at his sides as he listened to the sound of creaking wheels and men's voices coming from the road. Suddenly an Indian warwhoop split the air. Captain McLane shouted an order. Pistols cracked, muskets roared, and bowstrings twanged as the Continentals attacked the wagon train. Holding up his skirts, Sam stole closer to the road, longing to help his friends, even if it was only by throwing a snowball. But as quickly as it had begun, the fight was over. Horses pounded back up the road as the Tories fled. Captain McLane let them go. There were enough mouths to feed

188

already at Valley Forge without bringing in a bunch of prisoners.

The captain made a hasty inspection and found he had captured three wagons loaded with hams, barrels of flour, sacks of potatoes and other vegetables, besides eight beef cattle that had been driven along behind the wagons. Enough food to feed quite a few hungry Continental soldiers!

Watching from the edge of the road, Sam saw that there had been about ten Continental dragoons in the ambush and four Oneida scouts. Their gaunt horses were now led out of the woods, where they had been hidden. Some of the dragoons clambered up on the carts and got the convoy started for the American camp and one undertook to herd the cattle.

" 'Tis a fine welcome we'll receive across the Schuylkill tonight!" exclaimed one grinning, ragged trooper.

Captain McLane swung into his saddle. The pale winter sun was sliding down behind the trees and long blue shadows were creeping across the snowy road. The still leaves of the laurel rustled in a chilly breeze. The young captain frowned as he looked down at the forlorn picture made by Sam, standing beside the lonely road in his petticoats and hooded cloak.

In spite of his hurry to be off before some British band, roving the countryside, tried to recapture the convoy, he was loathe to ride away and leave a young girl alone in that desolate spot.

"Where are you bound for, sis?" he asked. "Hop up before me and I'll see you safely to your destination."

He reached down a hand to help Sam mount, but Sam, instead of clambering up to perch sideways before the captain, as any well-bred girl would do, hoisted his skirts and swung up behind him, astride the horse. Allan McLane seemed taken aback by such doings, and he looked even more surprised when Sam announced his destination.

"I'm on my way to Valley Forge. I've come from Philadelphia with an important message for General Washington."

The captain screwed his head around to take a close look at this strange girl. "Hmmm," he said thoughtfully. "Well, hold tight! I'll take you to headquarters, but I won't be easy on you if you're not telling the truth."

"General Washington will be glad to see me," Sam told him confidently.

It was a slow, cold ride because the horsemen couldn't move any faster than the wagons or cattle. Twilight was near by the time the troop arrived at the sturdy log bridge across the Schuylkill River. On the opposite bank of the river loomed the star-shaped fort that guarded this approach to the American camp. Captain McLane gave the password in reply to the ringing challenge of the sentry, and then led his dragoons with their convoy of wagons and beef cattle clattering, creaking, and thumping across the bridge.

A tingle ran down Sam's spine as they stepped off the bridge. At last he was at Valley Forge! He stared at the rows of log huts and at the gaunt, ragged soldiers, many of whom were dragging crude sleds piled with firewood that they had been cutting in the forest on the hills surrounding the camp. The Continental Army was in an even worse state than when Sam had seen it the year before. The men wore tattered blankets wrapped around them instead of coats; their feet were wrapped in blood-stained rags, and scarves tied over their ears framed frost-reddened faces. The Continental soldiers certainly were a horrible contrast to the spruce, well-clad British walking the streets of Philadelphia.

Yet the heroes of Valley Forge could still cheer Captain McLane and his captured supplies. And they inquired jokingly about the new recruit — the one riding behind the captain with her red petticoat hanging down under her blue coat.

"I didn't know you were that hard up for recruits, Allan!" yelled one soldier, who was using a crutch with one hand while he hauled a wood-laden sled with the other.

Their grins would be even wider, Sam thought happily, *if they knew what is quilted into this red petticoat.*

Captain McLane reined in his horse before an officer's log hut. "I must go in here for a moment," he told Sam. "Wait right where you are."

He ordered the rest of the troop to ride on to their own section of the camp, then dismounted and went into the hut to make his report.

As Sam watched the dragoons and the Indians ride away, he decided that he would try to join McLane's troop as a cook, horse boy, woodchopper, or in whatever capacity a recruit might be needed.

A young man wrapped in a black riding cloak was approaching on foot along the road, leading a limping horse. Sam guessed that they were bound for the blacksmith shop just ahead.

Suddenly he saw something familiar about them and muttered with dismay. He had recognized Tim Monroe and Chief. And here he sat in petticoats with curls peeping out under the frill of his wretched mobcap! Of all the terrible luck! Tim would never let him live this down.

As Tim came closer, he stared with frank curiosity at the girl astride a dragoon's horse, then lest he be considered rude, he lifted his hat respectfully. Sam's mouth opened in astonishment. Tim didn't know him! Suddenly his fear of being recognized was lost in his eagerness to get news of Joab, Mr. Leeds, and Tim himself. He slid off the horse on the side opposite Tim, hoping that if they spoke across the horse he still might escape recognition. But as he hit the ground his foot got tangled in his petticoat and he sat down hard in the snow beside the road.

Tim dropped Chief's reins and hurried to the help of the supposed girl. "Did you hurt yourself, miss? Let me assist you." He offered Sam his hand.

Sam kept his head down and bit his lip to keep from laughing. "Oh, fie, sir — you are too kind."

He allowed Tim to pull him to his feet. Tim looked a little surprised at the "girl's" weight, but he gallantly set about brushing snow off her cloak.

"I'll never be able to get back on that great beast," Sam murmured. "And I've still a long way to go."

"I'll lift you up, miss," Tim offered somewhat doubtfully. He put both hands at Sam's waist to swing him up.

"You are so strong!" Sam giggled.

" 'Tis nothing. You're as light as a fairy." Tim grew red in the face as he tried to hoist Sam. Sam had let himself become a deadweight and the gold in his petticoat added to the burden. Poor Tim panted and struggled to get him into the saddle, and at last Sam could contain his glee no longer. He exploded into ungirlish laughter. Tim let go of him and stepped back in amazement.

"Ha ha ha!" Sam shouted. " 'You're as light as a fairy!' Tim Monroe, I never knew that you were such a beau."

His hood fell back on his shoulders as he clutched at the horse to save himself from collapsing with mirth. Tim scowled ferociously as he recognized the face beneath the mobcap at last. "Sam Woodbury!"

"The same, sweet sir." Tears of laughter were rolling down Sam's cheeks. "I vow you're disappointed that I'm *not* a girl, you dandy!"

He grabbed Sam and the two boys began to struggle. Sam slipped and fell, dragging Tim down with him. They rolled across the road and were brought up in a snowdrift. Sam, hampered by his awkward clothes, found himself underneath. In spite of his wild efforts to break loose, he found himself pinned down by Tim, who got astride his chest. Tim picked up a handful of snow.

"I'm going to wipe that silly grin right off your face!" Tim growled.

Neither boy had noticed Captain McLane coming out of the cabin until a strong hand fastened on Tim's collar and dragged the angry boy to his feet.

"Are you daft, Tim Monroe? This is a nice way for a Congressional messenger to treat a girl."

Sam struggled to his feet. His mobcap was pushed over one ear and his cloak sagged off his shoulders, giving him a disreputable look. Eagerly he sought to set Tim right with the captain. "Tim and I were friends in Philadelphia," he explained.

"And he's no girl," Tim added sullenly. "He's Sam Woodbury, apprentice to old Leeds, the printer."

Captain McLane didn't look altogether surprised to discover that his prisoner wasn't a girl. Sam cut such a ridiculous figure that Tim had begun to laugh, in spite of himself, and the captain joined in. Sam tried to dig some snow out of his neck, then he grinned and held out his hand to Tim. "It's sure good to see you again, Tim."

The two boys shook hands warmly. "Why in the world are you gotten up in that outlandish outfit?" Tim asked.

"It's a long story. How's Joab? Is he here in camp?"

Tim nodded. "I stay in his hut whenever I bring dispatches to headquarters. Probably he can find room there for you too, if you plan to stay at camp. A couple of men assigned to that hut have been sent to the hospital."

Captain McLane interrupted. "You two can continue this conversation later. Come along — er — Sam. I'll take you to headquarters so you can deliver that important message to General Washington."

"I'd like to take off these clothes first," said Sam.

"There's no time for that," Captain McLane said crisply. "Besides, it's my duty to turn you over to the General exactly the way I found you." He swung up on his horse. "Come along!" he ordered.

Sam picked his basket out of the snow and pushed it into Tim's hands. "There's food in here. I'll see you and Joab soon, I hope."

He scrambled up behind Captain McLane.

"You're about as graceful as a moose," Tim chuckled. "I must have been crazy to have taken you for a girl."

Up the road, Captain McLane pulled up his horse in front of a stone house. "This is General Washington's headquarters," he said, as Sam slid to the ground. They walked to the front door, where Captain McLane gave his name to the guard on duty.

"Captain McLane and a messenger from Philadelphia for General Washington," he said to the officer who was at a table, looking over some papers. Sam recognized the handsome young officer in blue and buff as Captain McLane pushed him forward.

"Colonel Hamilton, this fellow claims to have an important message for the General."

The colonel's eyes widened. "*Fellow,* Captain McLane?"

"I'm Sam Woodbury, sir," Sam broke in. "I had to wear these clothes to get past the British lines." He pushed back his hood and snatched off the hated mobcap. At the sight of his boy's face, scarlet with embarrassment in the frame of sandy curls, the two young officers burst into roars of laughter.

"A fine-feathered bird indeed you've brought us, McLane," Colonel Hamilton gasped. Then he stopped laughing to take a keener look at Sam. "Sam Woodbury — " he murmured. "I know you now. You're the printer's apprentice who served with us at Trenton! You've a habit of turning up in odd ways, Sam."

A lady in a plain gray woolen gown and apron was hurrying down the stairs. Although short and plump, she had the look of a great lady.

"Gentlemen, what means this unseemly noise?" she scolded. "You will disturb the General." Her voice was stern but there was a twinkle in her blue eyes. Suddenly she became aware of Sam and stopped short in astonishment. "Well!" she exclaimed. "Well!"

"This is Sam Woodbury from Philadelphia, Mrs. Washington," Colonel Hamilton said, his eyes dancing.

Mrs. Washington looked so motherly that Sam found himself appealing to her.

"Oh, please, ma'am, help me out of these awful clothes! I couldn't stand to have General Washington see me like this. And besides, I've got to get this petticoat off so I can give the General the gold that is sewed into it."

Mrs. Washington and the two officers stared at him in amazement. "Did you say *gold?*" Colonel Hamilton demanded. "Gold in your petticoat?"

Sam nodded. "Mrs. Andrews quilted it between two layers of flannel. I used a pass that Mr. Andrews got for their granddaughter to go through the British lines — "

Mrs. Washington put her hand on his arm. "General Washington will want to hear this story," she said quietly. "Colonel, please ask the General to join us in my room."

Picking up his petticoats, Sam followed Mrs. Washington upstairs to her room. A young woman was sitting by the table, patching the seat of a large pair of buff breeches in the candlelight. Later, Sam was to learn that she was Lucy Knox, the wife of the General of Artillery, and that it was the General's saddle-worn breeches that she was patching.

Another chair stood by the table, and a ball of wool and a woolen stocking with knitting needles stuck into it showed that Mrs. Washington was also working for the soldiers.

"Come, Lucy, help me get these clothes off this boy," Mrs. Washington said briskly.

Mrs. Knox bubbled with laughter as she unbuttoned Sam's dress. "Goodness me, boy, how did you happen to get yourself rigged out like this?"

"I had to get out of Philadelphia," Sam said shortly. He was tired of being laughed at.

"Don't mind us, Sam," Mrs. Washington said, as if she could read his thoughts. "We admire the grit it took for you to come into camp dressed like a girl."

The dress fell to the floor and as Sam stepped out of it Mrs. Knox fell to laughing again. This time Sam joined in. He realized how funny he must look in the billowing red petticoat with his jacket showing above it.

"These clothes will come in very handy," Mrs. Washington declared, picking up the dress. "I'll use the dress and petticoat to make shirts for soldiers. And you'll need the cloak yourself, Sam, if you plan to stay on in camp."

"I couldn't return to Philadelphia while the British are there," Sam told her.

She gave him a confident smile. "Well then, Sam, you can return with General Washington in the spring."

Mrs. Knox untied the string of the petticoat. It klunked to the floor and Sam stepped out of it happily. At last he felt like a real boy again. He picked up the precious petticoat. Mrs. Knox took it from his hand.

"Glory!" she cried as she hefted its weight. "What makes it so heavy?"

Before Sam could reply, the door opened and General Washington stepped into the room, followed by Colonel Hamilton and Captain McLane. Sam squared his shoulders and stood as tall as he could. General Washington wasn't aware of it, but they had been comrades-in-arms at Trenton!

The General's piercing blue eyes met Sam's steady gray ones. "General," said Mrs. Washington, "this is Sam Woodbury. He has come from Philadelphia at some peril to himself to bring you something of which you have great need."

Sam took the petticoat from Mrs. Knox and pushed it into the hands of the surprised general. " 'Tis Mr. Milton's gold that I've fetched, sir," he said eagerly. "There are five thousand dollars in gold sewed into this petticoat."

Amazement at the amount of gold that he had brought held everyone silent for a few moments. Then the General smiled warmly.

"It's seldom that we receive such an interesting and welcome visitor," he told Sam. He turned to Mrs. Washington. "Where are your scissors, my dear? Let's have a look at this gold."

Colonel Hamilton got the scissors from Mrs. Washington's workbasket, and while the others crowded around, he cut two shimmering gold coins out of Sam's petticoat.

"Sam, you are a remarkable boy," Mrs. Washington said, hugging him.

General Washington took Sam's hand in his strong clasp. "Sam, I thank you in the name of all the men at Valley Forge, who so greatly need the food and medicine this gold will buy for them."

Sam was so proud that he felt that he must be standing as tall as General Washington himself. Suddenly he slumped a little. He was very tired, very hungry, and a long way from home.

Then he realized that Mrs. Washington's motherly voice was saying, "There's soup cooking in the kitchen for the General's supper. Let's you and I go down and sample it. After you have rested, the General, and all of us, will want to hear the story of your adventures."